PUFFIN

FLY BOY

ERIC WALTERS is the highly acclaimed and bestselling author of over seventy-five novels for children and young adults. His novels have won the Silver Birch Award and the Red Maple Award, as well as numerous other prizes, including the White Pine, Snow Willow, Tiny Torgi, Ruth Schwartz, and IODE Violet Downey Book Awards, and have received honours from the Canadian Library Association Book Awards, the Canadian Children's Book Centre, and UNESCO's international award for Literature in Service of Tolerance.

To find out more about Eric and his novels, or to arrange for him to speak at your school, visit his website at www.ericwalters.net.

ERIC WALTERS
FLY BOY

PUFFIN
an imprint of Penguin Canada

Published by the Penguin Group
Penguin Group (Canada), 90 Eglinton Avenue East, Suite 700, Toronto, Ontario, Canada M4P 2Y3
(a division of Pearson Canada Inc.)

Penguin Group (USA) Inc., 375 Hudson Street, New York, New York 10014, U.S.A.
Penguin Books Ltd, 80 Strand, London WC2R 0RL, England
Penguin Ireland, 25 St Stephen's Green, Dublin 2, Ireland (a division of Penguin Books Ltd)
Penguin Group (Australia), 250 Camberwell Road, Camberwell, Victoria 3124, Australia
(a division of Pearson Australia Group Pty Ltd)
Penguin Books India Pvt Ltd, 11 Community Centre, Panchsheel Park, New Delhi – 110 017, India
Penguin Group (NZ), 67 Apollo Drive, Rosedale, Auckland 0632, New Zealand (a division of Pearson New Zealand Ltd)
Penguin Books (South Africa) (Pty) Ltd, 24 Sturdee Avenue, Rosebank, Johannesburg 2196, South Africa

Penguin Books Ltd, Registered Offices: 80 Strand, London WC2R 0RL, England

Published in Puffin paperback by Penguin Canada, a division of Pearson Canada Inc., 2011

Published in this edition, 2012

3 4 5 6 7 8 9 10 (WEB)

Manufactured in Canada.

LIBRARY AND ARCHIVES CANADA CATALOGUING IN PUBLICATION

Walters, Eric, 1957–
Fly boy / Eric Walters.

ISBN 978-0-14-317631-2

I. Title.

PS8595.A598F59 2012   jC813'.54   C2011-908331-0

Visit the Penguin Canada website at **www.penguin.ca**

Special and corporate bulk purchase rates available; please see
www.penguin.ca/corporatesales or call 1-800-810-3104, ext. 2477.

ALWAYS LEARNING   **PEARSON**

FOR THOSE GALLANT MEN AND WOMEN—

MANY OF WHOM ARE NOW GONE—

WHO GAVE OF THEMSELVES TO SAVE DEMOCRACY

FOREWORD

The action within this story takes place at a time when the powers of good and evil stood face to face, eyeball to eyeball, each side convinced that victory in World War Two was within its grasp. The aircrews on both sides were pawns in a sinister game, their leaders locked in a power struggle to the death. Unconditional surrender was the only acceptable solution for either side.

We in Bomber Command were well aware that every time we left the deck, some of us would live, some would die. While the majority of us were around the age of twenty-one, sadly fifty percent of us never lived to see twenty-two. As *Fly Boy* makes clear, experience and skill may have helped in our legendary struggle for survival, but these were not the only factors contributing to success. Most of it came down to Lady Luck.

The air war in World War Two knew no end, no hesitation. Each and every day, by daylight and by darkness, we flew our heavy bombers forth from the runways. Flying by night, we'd get the wild idea that we were the only ones out there—until we neared the target. Suddenly the dangers would come into full view. There would be bombs going down, varying calibres of anti-aircraft fire coming back up, spoofs exploding, bombers colliding, fighter flares erupting, factories on fire, tracer bullets slicing every which way, unfortunate Lancasters being bombed from above, aircraft—theirs and ours—going down in flames, and the inevitable swarm of searchlights probing everywhere, never resting until they found a victim.

To me it was the nearest thing to hell on earth that I had ever seen. And yet, as operations continued, we found ourselves actually becoming accustomed to the outrage—accepting the explosions, the carnage, the noise, and the smells as routine. Most frightening of all, we were becoming really good at our jobs.

But while the results we achieved were impressive, the price we paid was horrendous. On one occasion, as I secured myself into the pilot's seat of a Lancaster bomber, I remember thinking, *Am I really the same shy little boy from the northeast of Scotland who, just the day before yesterday, was racing barefoot across a farmer's field, knees skinned, pants ripped, trying to catch a rabbit? What is this war doing to me?*

Read along with *Fly Boy* and feel what we felt, see what we saw, live what we lived. Eric has perfectly captured the spirit of the war days, when the future of the world was in the balance and we had no choice but to go forward.

Flight Lieutenant Philip Gray, AEA
186 and 622 Squadrons
Bomber Command

Philip Gray's riveting account of his days in Bomber Command can be found in his book *Ghosts of Targets Past* (Grub Books), which is available at bookstores, through Amazon.ca, or by contacting the author directly at philip.gray@sympatico.ca to receive a personalized copy.

I stared out of the train window and watched as the countryside passed by. It looked so calm and prosperous and peaceful. But why shouldn't it? The war was half a continent and a full ocean away in either direction.

Chip slumped into a seat across from mine. "I found this in the club car," he said. He had a newspaper in his hands. "It's yesterday's *Toronto Daily Star*."

"What are the headlines?"

He held up the front page. Under the date—September 2, 1943—the large black type read ALLIES SLICE THROUGH SICILY! and beneath that was a photograph of a Tiger tank rolling past a destroyed building.

"We've been gaining ground, especially since the Americans entered the war, but the Germans still have a lot of fight in them," Chip said.

"A lot less fight than if they hadn't tried to take on Russia as well," I said. "It's just a matter of time, now, until we invade France and start taking it back."

"Yeah, and with our luck, it will probably all be over before we're even old enough to enlist."

"Hard to say," I muttered.

"Don't get me wrong," he went on. "Of course I want the war to be over, to beat the Nazis ... but still, I don't want to miss my chance to be part of it."

"You're preaching to the choir, buddy," I said.

"Just think—we only have to put up with one more year of boarding school before we can enlist together next summer, when we both turn eighteen ... like we promised we would."

This was getting harder. Chip had been my best friend forever, and I couldn't help feeling like a bit of a rat. I took a deep breath.

"What if I told you that I can't keep that promise?"

"What are you talking about?" Chip looked puzzled. "You're the only person I know who wants to enlist even more than I do. Is it your mother? I know it's hard on her, what with your father and all."

My father was a Spitfire pilot, and he'd been shot down and taken prisoner. It was terrible knowing he was a prisoner of war, but at least we knew he was safe, and the monthly letters we received confirmed that.

"My mother's not so crazy about the idea either," Chip

admitted. "But you know, Robbie, you will be eighteen, an *adult*, so really, if you want to enlist, she can't stop you."

"It's not that she'll stop me," I said. "Actually, she'll be far too late to even try to stop me."

"What are you babbling on about?"

We were less than thirty minutes out of Toronto now. I'd put it off as long as I could—but that just made it harder now.

"What if I told you … I won't have to wait a year to be part of the fighting?" I asked.

"I'd tell you to quit kidding around."

Even if I told him, he wasn't going to believe me. I reached into my pocket and pulled out the papers and handed them to him.

"What are these?"

"My enlistment papers."

"Your *what?*" he yelled.

Heads all around the car turned toward us.

"Keep your voice down," I hissed at him. "Those are my enlistment papers. I joined the Royal Canadian Air Force."

"That's not possible. You're not old enough!"

"Keep your voice *down*," I said again.

"Oh … sorry."

"You're holding the proof in your hands. Remember

last month when I went down to Toronto to see my sick great-aunt?"

"I remember. I thought it was kind of odd. You don't even like her very much."

"I don't, but I needed an excuse to get away."

"So you didn't visit your great aunt?"

"Of course I did, but that wasn't the only reason I went to Toronto. I went down to enlist."

"If you wanted to enlist, you could have just gone down to Kingston. It's so much closer to home," Chip said.

"That's *why* I didn't. I wanted to go someplace where I was less likely to bump into anybody who knew me," I explained. "Besides, I had other business to take care of."

"But I don't get it. Even if they didn't know you, they would still know from your ID that you're only seventeen and not eligible to enlist."

"*I'm* only seventeen, but not my brother."

"Your brother is eleven years old, so how would that help?" he asked.

"Not my *younger* brother, my *older* brother."

"You don't have an older brother!" Chip exclaimed. "You've got one brother and two sisters, and you're the oldest kid in your family."

"I am the oldest, but I wasn't the firstborn. My parents'

first child, David James McWilliams, was born a year earlier than me. He only lived a few days, but he was born and baptized, and I used those papers to enlist."

I opened the papers to show him the name. His eyes widened in shock as he read. "Robbie, you can't just—"

"Please," I said, cutting him off. "It would be better if you called me David. I need to get accustomed to my new name."

He took a deep breath. He wasn't happy about this. "*David*, I just—"

"No, that's wrong ... far too formal. How about Dave, or maybe Davie? Yes, that's it, Davie! You're my oldest friend, so you'd probably call me Davie!"

He reached across and put a hand on my shoulder. "Robert," he said very formally, looking me straight in the eyes. "Even if you *did* manage to fool some 4-F recruiting officer with thick glasses and bad eyesight into believing that you're eighteen, how long do you think it'll be before your mother finds out that you're gone?"

"I *am* gone—to boarding school."

"And she'll find out soon enough that you're not there. How long before the headmaster contacts her to ask why you're not in attendance at school? Do you really think old Beamish is so daft that he won't notice you're not there?"

"He knows I'm not there. That was the other business I took care of when I was in Toronto. I went to the school and explained to him that I wouldn't be able to attend this year because of financial issues … you know, what with my father being a POW, and things being hard for my mother and all."

"And he believed you?"

"Well, I think he believed the letter from my mother explaining everything."

"Your mother wrote a *letter*?"

"Of course not, you idiot! I wrote the letter and forged her signature."

"I don't know if that's insanity or genius," Chip said.

"They say there's a fine line between the two, and I hope I'm standing on the right side of it."

"But what about letters between you and your mother?" he asked. "You know the first time she writes to you—her son who's in school—she'll know something is wrong."

"Aren't you in charge of the mailroom as part of your punishment for that prank we played on Mr. Henderson?"

"A prank that only I got caught doing and … Oh, I get it, so I can intercept the letters! Is that what you're saying?"

"Exactly. The headmaster won't be bothered by what he doesn't see. What he doesn't know won't hurt *me*."

"But as you might recall, I'm only being punished the first few months of the year. What happens after December?"

"I was sort of hoping you could do something else wrong and get the punishment extended until the end of the school year."

"You can't expect me to deliberately try to get into ... Wait, that's probably going to end up happening one way or another, isn't it?"

"Of course it will. I'm simply counting on you to get in your usual amount of trouble."

"Without you there, it just won't have the same magic to it, but I'll do my best," he said with a grin. "Now, that just leaves one problem. What about your letters to your mother? It's not like you can send letters postmarked from England, and I know she's not going to let you go a whole school year without writing."

I reached over and unsnapped my valise and pulled out three envelopes. Each was stamped, addressed to my mother, and contained a letter. I turned one of the envelopes over and opened up the flap.

"You see here, this number I wrote in pencil?"

"Yes."

"I've numbered the letters one, two, and three. You just need to mail them to my mother in that order. One each month for the next three months. Just erase the little number, seal them off, and send them. Each letter talks a little bit about how wonderfully the school year is going, how much I'm enjoying classes, and in October I'm going to be coming down with a cold and will have to miss a rugby game ... I'm going to be terribly disappointed."

"You are definitely moving to the genius side of the line, my friend! But what then? What happens after the third letter is mailed?"

"By then I'll be in a place where you can send me letters, with her letters to me inside, and I'll send you back letters with a new letter to her tucked inside that envelope. And of course, in your letters, you'll give me enough information about school and events that I'll be able to fill in the details in my letters to her. I think I have all the bases covered."

"And if Mommy decides to come and pay you a visit? Won't she be in for a nasty surprise when you're not there?"

"Chip, my mother hasn't been able to come to Toronto since my father enlisted. She's stuck at home looking after my brother and sisters. She's lucky if she gets a chance to go over to the neighbour's for coffee."

"I guess you have all the bases covered for the school year, but what about in July when you're supposed to return home?"

"I'm going to be writing my mother throughout the year explaining that if I do extremely well in school, there will be an opportunity for me to stay on during the summer and be a paid tutor for some of the younger students. She's going to be so proud of me!" I beamed.

"And after that?"

"And after that I'll be eighteen, and I'll just tell her I've enlisted, and there will be nothing she can do about it. She'll know I'm in the air force, but she won't know that I've already been there for ten months."

Chip shook his head slowly and a smile came to his face. "I'm jealous! And I must admit that I'm a little bit hurt that you didn't bring me in on the plan before this."

"I'm sorry, Chip. I just didn't want to drag you too far into this. There's going to be hell to pay if this gets out, and I didn't want you to be implicated too deeply. I want you to at least try to plead ignorance."

"Ignorance has always been my best defence! But you're right—I know the military needs everyone who can to enlist, but I imagine they're not very understanding about people enlisting under a false identity. You could be in really big trouble."

"I'm just hoping that by the time they find out I'll be such a hotshot ace pilot that they'll be happy to look the other way, because they need pilots so badly."

He reached out his hand. "My congratulations, sir. You've thought of everything."

"I tried. Which leaves me with one more favour to ask of you." I reached into my valise and handed him a fourth envelope. "Inside is a letter from Headmaster Beamish confirming for the air force that I've completed my junior matriculation, graduating with both high honours and distinction."

Chip opened the envelope and took out the letter. It was typed and had the headmaster's signature at the bottom. "This is official school stationery. How did you get this?" Chip asked.

"This summer when I was in Beamish's office and told him I wasn't returning to school, I got rather choked up. He turned to get me a handkerchief, and when he wasn't looking, I pinched a couple of sheets."

"I think you're wasting your time wanting to be a pilot. You should be a secret agent."

"I'll take that as a compliment. Just pop it in the mail so it's clear from the postmark that it was sent from the school. Okay?"

"I'll do whatever I can to help out. You can count on me."

"More than anybody else I know. You're a good friend," I said.

"And at the end of the year," Chip replied, "when I turn eighteen and enlist, maybe we'll even end up in the same unit."

"That could happen. Of course, I don't know if we could be friends," I said.

"What do you mean?" He looked a bit shocked.

"Well, by then I'll be a full-fledged ace, and you'll just be a *sprog*."

"Sprog ... What's a sprog?"

"New pilot, fresh out of training, wet behind the ears, with no combat missions to your credit!"

"Oh, yeah? Well, I'll still be a sprog who's big enough to box your ears!" Chip growled.

"Oh, sure! Try hitting a superior officer and see where that gets you! Time in the can and—"

"Next stop, Union Station!" the conductor announced as he walked down the aisle of the car. "Next stop, Union Station, Toronto!"

"That's our—I mean, *my* stop," Chip said. "I wish we had more time to talk."

"We do have a little more time. I'm getting off here too," I said.

"Your training is in Toronto?"

"Not my training, my *train*. I have to meet up with the rest of the fellows who've enlisted and catch the train from here. You can walk me to my platform."

2

The train shuddered and then came to a stop. We both got up and shuffled down the aisle along with everybody else, dragging our luggage with us. I'd been told not to bring much with me, just what I could fit in my valise, but Chip had everything he'd need for a year at boarding school, including his tennis racquet, lacrosse stick, and winter coat and boots.

"My train leaves from platform four in about an hour," I said.

"Where are you going to?"

"Brandon, Manitoba."

"Manitoba! I've heard about winters on the Prairies. You're going to freeze to death!"

"Not likely. I'm only there for basic training, about a month, so I'll be long gone before winter arrives."

"Long gone to where?"

"That's the question. I could be assigned to any one of the

air training schools across the country, depending on how well I do."

"What do you mean?" Chip asked.

"Some of the schools are for pilots, others specialize in training navigators, or bomb aimers, or wireless operators."

"Oh, you'll be a pilot—no question! You know more about airplanes than anybody I ever met."

"Knowing about them doesn't make you a pilot."

"Yeah, I guess ... but I can see you flying ... Spitfires, like your father."

"I can only hope."

We made our way through the crowds on the platform, jumped down onto the tracks, and crossed over two more sets of tracks to platform four. There were only a few people there—a woman with a child, and an old man at the far side—and none of them looked as if they might be on their way to report for training.

We both tossed our bags up and then climbed up onto the platform.

"You sure you haven't missed it?" Chip asked.

I looked at my watch. "It's due in less than thirty minutes."

"Thirty minutes ... so you still have time to change your mind."

"It's too late for that."

"As far as I can tell, it won't be too late for thirty-*one* minutes."

"No. Maybe the train isn't here yet, but that ship has already sailed. I've got a boarding school that isn't expecting me and a recruiting officer who is. What do you think will happen if David James McWilliams doesn't report for duty?"

"Not much, I'd guess, since he's already been dead and buried for eighteen years."

"But when they do come looking for *him*, they're going to find *me*, and that's where the trouble will begin. I have no choice."

"I guess you're right. Stand up straighter," he said, poking me in the side.

I straightened up. "I'll stand at attention when I need to."

"You need to all the time. You're kinda short, you know."

"Thanks for pointing that out. Real nice."

"I'm not trying to be nice or not nice. I'm just trying to tell you that you need to stand up, throw back your shoulders, and try to look older."

"I started to grow a moustache."

"You what?"

"I started to grow a moustache," I repeated.

"I don't see *anything*."

"See?" I turned my head slightly to the side.

"Oh, yeah … there it is. It should come in good—in about four years."

"It's coming. It's just that I'm fair haired and it's harder to see."

"*Impossible* to see without a microscope. Between that peach fuzz and the baby face, you hardly pass for sixteen, let alone eighteen."

"Lots of people don't look their ages. I have the papers to *prove* I'm eighteen. Once I grow a moustache, nobody will question me."

"Forget about growing a moustache—maybe you should just try to grow a few inches taller."

"That could happen," I said defensively. "My father told me he wasn't very big until he hit twenty."

"Your father?" Chip said. "Your father is big."

"He's not that much more than six feet tall."

"Yeah, but he's big, you know, lots of muscles, and I can't imagine he ever had your little baby face, even when he was born."

"This isn't the sort of support I was hoping for."

"I'm sorry. You're right. You just have to understand that this is all sort of sudden. Thirty minutes ago we're heading back to boarding school together, and now I'm waiting for you to board a train to go to air school."

"It does take some getting used to," I agreed. "I've been thinking about this for a long time, and I enlisted a whole month ago, but in some ways, it didn't actually seem real to me until I told you."

I looked down the platform. It was starting to get more crowded. There were men—some looked not much older than me—either standing on their own or with a girlfriend or wife. Some of them even had kids with them. Those men were a *lot* older than me.

"I'm going to miss you," Chip said.

"To be honest, I expect I'm going to be too busy to miss *you* very much."

"I understand. But you'd better write, a lot, and not just the letters to keep your mother in the dark. You write and tell me what's really happening, all the time."

"Now you sound like my sweetie or my wife. You're not going to try to kiss me goodbye, are you?" I asked with a smirk.

"I might *kick* you goodbye if you give me any more of your lip."

I held up my hands. "No more. I need you too much."

I looked down the tracks. There was a train, smoke billowing from its stack, making its way into the station. Its brakes squealed, and the engine spewed out excess steam as it slowed down and slid to a stop alongside the platform.

"I think this is it," I said. For some reason, just then I was finding it kind of hard to breathe.

A soldier—no, an airman, I could tell by his light blue uniform—was standing in the middle of the platform, and he started calling out names from a list he was holding. For each name, a man came forward, bag in hand, and reported in, and his name was ticked off the list. The names were in alphabetical order, so I'd be somewhere in the middle.

There were lots of hugs and kisses and tears before each man climbed onto the train. Then, one by one, windows opened as men who had already boarded leaned down and kept talking or clasped the hands of their loved ones still on the platform. I suddenly wished my mother were here, or my brother or sisters, or that I had a girlfriend who would be broken up by my leaving. All I had was Chip. Still, I imagined that was better than just standing there by myself.

"McWilliams, David James!" the airman yelled.

"Okay, I'm off," I said to Chip. "Take care of those letters for me."

"I'll take care of everything at this end. Just don't go getting yourself killed."

"Not planning on it."

"Do you want the top or bottom bunk?"

"It doesn't matter to me."

"In that case, how about I take the bottom and you take the top." He held out his hand. "I'm Jim Casey."

"Good to meet you. I'm—" I stopped short just as I was going to call myself Robbie. "I'm David McWilliams, but my friends call me Dave."

"Good to meet you, Dave. My guess is, before this is over, we're going to need all the friends we can get."

"I think you might be right."

The train shuddered forward a foot and stopped, and I stumbled, grabbing the back of the seat to keep my balance. It then started slowly pulling out of the station.

"Looks like we're getting going," Jim said. He slumped down in his seat.

I went over to the window and searched for Chip. I couldn't see him amongst the mass of crying, waving people on the platform. Maybe he'd already left.

"Wife or girlfriend?" Jim asked.

"I'm a little young for a wife," I said.

"Figured if you were old enough to fight, you were old enough to marry. One battle is as rough as the other."

"Just a friend who came down to see me off, but I think he's gone. You?"

"I said goodbye to my mother and girlfriend this morning. I didn't see any point in them coming down here to shed more tears."

I guess that made sense, and there really wasn't any point in Chip waiting around any—

"There he is!"

Chip was standing on a bench, so he was head and shoulders above the crowd. He had one hand above his eyes and was trying to peer into the cars. I opened the window, leaned out, and waved as we chugged by.

"Be safe!" Chip yelled.

"You too!" I called back before I realized just how stupid that sounded.

I turned and watched as we picked up speed and left him farther behind. I kept watching as he got smaller and smaller, but he kept on waving until finally he jumped down from his perch and disappeared into the crowd.

I sat down in the seat opposite Jim's. This was all happening. This was all real. I was leaving behind everything I'd known. I suddenly felt very small and very alone.

"Here." Jim was holding out a small silver flask.

"What is it?"

"Whisky. Have a shot."

I hesitated.

"Don't worry, it's good stuff. No rotgut."

I took the flask and tipped it back and took a little sip. It tasted awful and burned all the way down my throat. I handed him back the flask.

"Probably not the best you've ever tasted," he said.

"But not the worst either," I lied.

He held the flask up. "To new adventures and new friends!" He tipped it back and took a big slug.

Maybe I didn't like his whisky, but it was good not to be so alone. To new adventures and new friends.

3

"Not much to look at," Jim said.

"Nothing but fields of wheat since we left northern Ontario, except for Winnipeg … I wish we could have gotten out to look around."

"I wish we could have just gotten off the train for good. Two days is too long to be riding the rails."

"It's been a long time," I agreed.

The motion of the train had made Jim sick—not the best thing for somebody who wanted to be a pilot—but I'd actually enjoyed the ride. I'd never been west of Toronto before, and I would have stayed awake the whole time if I could have.

"Not much longer, at least," Jim said.

I looked at my watch. "Less than ten minutes."

The sergeant had come through twenty minutes ago to tell us to get all our gear packed and be ready to disembark in thirty minutes.

"It's so empty out here," Jim said. "Hardly any people at all, just a few scattered houses in the distance."

"I think that's why the training school is out here, so it can be away from everybody."

"Makes sense," he agreed.

Over the two days, I'd gotten to know a lot of the other guys. There were over three hundred men, and they could be divided into two groups: older guys, some even in their thirties, who were married, with kids, and younger, single guys, some not much older than me or Jim. Jim was only nineteen, but big enough to easily pass for a year or two older. Once the train had gotten underway, the two groups quickly separated, with people even shifting their sleeping berths so they would be on different cars of the train.

Both groups had done a lot of loud talking, card playing, shooting craps, and drinking. Especially drinking. Jim wasn't the only one with a flask. Bottles seemed to materialize out of nowhere, and I got the feeling that some people had brought along more booze than they had clothing. I'd even heard that a couple of guys had almost been left behind in Winnipeg when they'd dashed off the train to run to the liquor store to replenish their supplies.

I'd had a couple of sips from Jim's flask, but nothing more.

Neither of my parents were drinkers, and there wasn't any alcohol in our house. It had never really appealed much to me, and now, after spending two days on a train with some guys who couldn't hold their liquor or their tempers, I was even less tempted to take up the habit.

There'd been more than a few arguments, and at least twice, when push came to shove, a couple of guys were ready to have a set-to. The nearby presence of the sergeants and the calmer heads of others kept things from heating up any further.

The other thing that seemed to occupy time for a lot of the guys was gambling. I'd seen them trying to play craps—dice—but the movement of the train kept interfering with the rolling of the dice, but they still played, trying to compensate for the train's movement tipping the dice one way or another. Instead, there were lots of card games going on. I'd never played cards before—at least not for money—and a lot of bills were on the table.

My money—my *parents'* money to pay for my year in boarding school—was safe, squirrelled away in a sock at the bottom of my bag. I felt bad about even having it, but I had to take it with me. It would have been pretty hard to explain to my mother why she didn't need to pay tuition for my schooling that year. When this was all over, I'd just give them back the money. Besides, it wasn't bad to have a little extra cash, just in case.

When I wasn't looking out the window at the scenery, I just stood off to one side and watched the games being played. I'd found that was the safest place, because some of the guys got antsy when you stood behind them, as if they thought you were giving signals and helping somebody cheat them.

I'd already been asked about my age. It wasn't just that I was younger, I really *looked* younger. A couple of the older guys had been giving me a hassle about being so young when Jim walked by. He just told them that guys like me and him were brave enough to "enlist as soon as we could," not like some "lily-livered zombies" who had to be drafted. Calling somebody a zombie was about the worst insult you could give, and for a few seconds it looked as if Jim had only helped me get into a fight. But then they'd smiled and laughed and offered us both a drink from their flasks.

I knew I had to start doing things that would at least make me *seem* older. The moustache thing wasn't going to work. Other guys had had to shave a couple of times during the trip, but I could practically have used a face cloth to wipe away the peach fuzz that was starting to form on my upper lip.

I thought about taking up smoking, but trying that for the first time might even make the situation worse. What if I started to cough when I lit up or, worse, turned green and threw up, the way I'd seen some guys do? The thick haze of smoke that hung in the air was almost enough to make me feel sick, and a couple of times I'd had to go outside between cars to catch some fresh air.

I felt the train start to slow down, and I could see a few small houses out the window. We were obviously on the outskirts of Brandon. As we continued to slow down, more and more houses and even stores appeared, until we finally pulled up to the station. There was no elevated platform here, but there were trucks—RCAF trucks—waiting beside the tracks.

The train shuddered to a final stop. It would be good to get my feet back on solid—

"Move it, move it, move it!" screamed one of the sergeants. "Do you men think this is the start of your vacation? Get your butts off this train and onto those trucks, double time!"

There was a mad scramble as men jumped to their feet, grabbed their bags from the luggage compartments, and pushed forward to get off the train. I wedged myself in behind Jim and joined a stream of men flooding down the aisle and out the door, leaping to the ground.

The tailgates of the trucks were down, and we tossed our bags in one truck and climbed up. There were benches on both sides, and we plopped down on the hard wooden seats. It filled up quickly, and then a couple of airmen lifted the tailgate and slammed it closed with a loud thud that shook the whole vehicle. They then pulled the canvas flaps closed, blocking most of the view. I felt a little claustrophobic, stuffed in with twenty other men, sitting shoulder to shoulder, my knees almost touching the person facing me. Quickly it started to get hot and stuffy in there.

"What are they waiting for?" somebody asked. There was a hint of both annoyance and anxiety in his voice. Maybe I wasn't the only one feeling uncomfortable.

Almost on cue, the engine started and the whole truck began rumbling. The little bit of fresh air that had managed to get through the opening in the back was replaced by exhaust fumes. The truck started forward and we rocked from side to side. The ride wasn't smooth, but at least we were leaving behind the smell of the exhaust.

"Anybody have any idea how far away the camp is?" somebody asked.

There were mumbled responses that varied from "Wouldn't think too far" to "An hour or two," so really nobody had any idea. It didn't matter. We were going wherever they were taking us, and there wasn't anything we could do about it short of jumping out of the back— and judging from the increasing speed of the truck, that wasn't much of an option either. I just knew that the faster we drove, the faster we'd get there, and that was fine by me.

I caught little glimpses of the world as it passed, of houses and stores. Paved roads gave way to hard-packed gravel. Behind us was another military truck, and when we hit a curve, I could see a second and third and fourth before the turn blocked my view. Since there had been three hundred of us on the train and each truck held around twenty men, there had to be about fifteen vehicles in this convoy.

The truck's brakes squealed, slowing it down dramatically before a sharp turn, and a cloud of dust was kicked up—by us and whatever vehicles were in front of us. I was suddenly glad the flap was almost completely closed. The road—the dirt road—was much rougher, and we rocked and bumped our way along slowly. I gripped the bench with both hands to stop myself from bouncing off. Finally we came to a stop.

Almost instantly I could hear doors opening and men yelling. Our flap was pulled back and then the tailgate opened up.

"All of you out, out, out!" screamed an airman.

Again we jumped to our feet and we scrambled out of the trucks, moving awkwardly, bumping bodies and bags as we leaped to the ground.

"Form up in two, I repeat, *two* rows!" screamed a sergeant. "Tallest in the back and shortest in the front!" He looked at Jim. "You're in the back, Stretch." Then at me. "And you, son, are definitely in the very front row … We might even want to start a special row just for you!"

A few people started to laugh.

"The rest of you button it up. I'm not here to amuse you!" he screamed. "Is there anybody here who thinks I'm amusing?"

Everybody shut up quickly, put their heads down, and tried to assemble into rows. It wasn't that easy a task as two rows of about a hundred and fifty men each kept shifting and squirming, trying to fit everybody in. Men bumped into each other and exchanged a few unpleasantries.

I settled into the middle of the front row—almost directly in front of three sergeants standing there glowering at us—and Jim was directly behind me. I would have liked to have been behind him so I could be completely hidden.

"Come on, double time!" yelled the sergeant—the one who had insulted me. "Come on, *ladies*, how are we to expect any of you to learn to fly if you don't even know how to stand in two rows?"

Finally, after what seemed like forever but was only a few minutes, we were all standing in our rows.

"Attention!" came the order.

Immediately all bags were dropped to the ground and we stood at attention.

"At ease," came the next order, and we relaxed—at least slightly.

"Good morning, gentlemen! My name is Flight Warrant Officer Crowly." He started pacing in front of us. "I have been asked by our commanding officer to welcome you to Manning Depot Number Two, situated in *beautiful* Brandon, Manitoba. He would have welcomed you himself, but he is *far* too busy and *far* too important to *waste* his time on a bunch of raw recruits. And if I do say so myself, you are one of, if not *the* most pathetic group I have ever had the misfortune to greet!"

I knew that some of them—after two days of drinking, gambling, and not sleeping or shaving—did look pretty rough.

"I knew that as the war went on, we'd find ourselves *scraping* the bottom of the barrel, but in this group I see men who might actually be the *barrel* itself!" he yelled. "Or in some cases, if not the bottom of the barrel, only recently out of the crib!"

He suddenly stopped and spun around right in front of me. "Just how old are you, son?"

"I'm eighteen, sir ... I mean Flight Officer!" I yelled back.

"I see that you already know I'm not a 'sir,' but you'd better get it right. It is Flight *Warrant* Officer! Do you understand that, son?" he demanded.

"Yes, Flight Warrant Officer!" I answered.

"Do you all understand?" he screamed.

"Yes, Flight Warrant Officer!" came back a chorus of replies.

"Only officers are to be addressed as 'sir,' although you will salute anybody who outranks you, and gentlemen, *everybody* outranks you! You are the lowest of the low, aircraftman two, an acey-deucey."

So that's what that meant.

"While there may be a lower form of life on this planet, it has not yet been found by science. You will salute *everything*. If you pass a cow or a pig, you should salute it because at this point it is making a larger contribution to the war effort than you are! Am I understood?"

"Yes, Flight Warrant Officer!" people yelled.

"Manning Depot is your first stop, one of over two hundred schools scattered throughout the world that make up the British Commonwealth Air Training Plan. In total our schools graduate over three thousand airmen each month. Hopefully more than a few of you men will surprise me and actually graduate. By a show of hands, how many of you want to become pilots?"

My hand went up, as did almost every hand around me.

"What a shock that the acey-deucies all want to become pilots. Well, gentlemen, and I use that term very loosely, you are probably not aware of this, but most of you will *not* become pilots. And do you know why?"

I didn't think he was looking for an answer, but I was sure he was going to tell us.

"Because while it may seem that flying is magical, airplanes do not fly on magic. You there, boy," he said, pointing at me once again. "Do you still believe in the Easter Bunny, or Santa Claus?"

"No, Flight Warrant Officer!"

"How about pixies and fairies? Do you believe in them?"

"No, Flight Warrant Officer!" I bellowed, trying desperately to make my voice sound louder and deeper.

"Even this little baby, not long from the crib, who not long ago couldn't sleep Christmas Eve waiting for Santa to bring him a shiny new bicycle—even *he* knows there's no magic. We can't all just become pilots and sprinkle pixie dust on the wings to make the plane fly. For a plane to fly, it needs ground crew that can fix the engines and fuel the aircraft. It does no good to fly a plane if you don't know where it's going—it needs navigators. There's no point in knowing where you're going if you don't have gunners to protect the plane along the route. There is no point in being protected and knowing where to go if you can't do something when you get there—that's why we need bomb aimers. *All* of these jobs are equally important, and over the next four weeks we will determine just which of those jobs is right for you!"

He could say what he wanted—I *knew* what I was going to be, and there was nothing he could say that would convince me differently.

"I know what's going on in your heads," he said. "You figure I don't know what I'm saying, that you're going to become a pilot."

I had the strangest feeling that he *was* reading my mind.

"And that's what all of you are thinking. But I'm right and you're wrong. You'd better get that straight right now, because you're going to soon find out that I'm *always* right and you're *always* wrong."

The other two sergeants nodded in agreement.

"When you are dismissed, you are to go inside the barracks, find an empty bunk, drop off your bags, and report back out here for an initial orientation meeting. You have ten minutes to do that. I repeat, *ten minutes*. Not eleven, not twelve, *ten*. Dismissed!" he yelled.

We stampeded into the barracks. The ceilings soared overhead, the floors were bare concrete, and there was a strange odour.

"What is that smell?" I asked.

"I think it's two smells," Jim said. "Disinfectant, maybe bleach, is one smell, and it's there to cover up the other smell, which, as a farm boy, I'm very familiar with. It's manure."

"Manure! But why would it ..." I let the sentence trail off as it all made sense. I realized what our barracks had actually been.

We were being housed in a building that used to hold livestock. In the centre there was a large open space extending up thirty or forty feet, probably where the show ring or arena had been, and there were hundreds and hundreds of bunk beds that had taken the place of the animal stalls. They'd removed the bars and boards and replaced them with beds, but the smell still lingered. We weren't going to be sleeping in a barn but in a gigantic cow palace, a place where animals were exhibited at a fall fair.

Most of the beds were already in use, but we came to a whole section where the beds were unmade—blankets and sheets and pillows piled up at the end. We grabbed a bunk bed and Jim dropped his pack onto the bottom bunk while I tossed my valise up onto the top. For a second I thought about all that money in the bottom of my bag, but really there wasn't time to do anything about it.

We got back outside in time to see that a line had already formed. Two airmen stood at the front, handing something out. We had no idea what it was for or about, but we knew enough to join in at the end, which quickly expanded as other "acey-deucies" settled in behind us.

"Gentlemen!" a sergeant yelled as he walked down the line. "You will receive a checklist when you get to the front of the line. On that list are seventy steps that you must complete before the day is out. Each of these steps is necessary and important. You can start at step number one and work your way through the list sequentially, but all that is important is that you complete all of the steps, not the order of the steps. Upon completion of each step, it will be duly initialled by the responsible airman. Do I make myself clear?"

cap. The airman took the sheet and put his initials beside the appropriate lines to show that I'd been issued each part of my uniform.

I shuffled sideways to the next counter, where boots were being distributed.

"Size seven," I said.

"Is that adult or children's size he's taking?" the airman two over said loudly, and his buddy beside him at the counter laughed.

I'd just about had enough. And I knew enough about both bullies and being smaller to know that this had to stop now.

"My feet are big enough to kick your butt!" I said.

The laughter stopped—as did all the other sounds around us. Nobody was talking or joking around any longer. Everybody was watching. A couple of the airmen between the two of us stepped aside. The guy who had made the comment wasn't much older than me ... but he was bigger.

"What's wrong, buddy? You can't take a little friendly joking around?" he asked.

"Get it right, you *aren't* my friend."

The man chuckled nervously. This wasn't what he'd expected.

"We both came here to train to fight the Nazis," I said. "I'd rather we don't have to fight each other ... but I will if I have to."

"No offence, kid, I was just—"

"I'm *not* a kid. I'm an aircraftman two, an acey-deucey, just like you." I stepped forward and held out my hand. "David McWilliams."

"John McNabb," he said as we shook.

"My friends call me Davie. Starting from now on, you can call me Davie."

John smiled. "I get Johnnie. Pleased to meet you, Davie."

The corporals behind the counter brought back some boots—a pair for me and another pair for Johnnie. I noticed that my new friend's boots didn't look much bigger than my sevens.

I started to try on the boots.

"Keep moving!" the corporal barked. "If they fit or don't fit, it doesn't matter. You asked for sevens and that's what you got."

The corporal initialled my sheet and we quickly moved off again.

"What's next on the list?" Jim asked.

I looked down at the sheet. I didn't like the look of it. The next five spaces simply said *Inoculations*—shots.

We followed behind the men leaving the area carrying their uniforms and newly issued boots. I looked at Jim's new boots. They were so enormous I wondered if they'd even fit in the cockpit of a plane. Actually, would *Jim* fit in a cockpit?

Of course, I'd never been in the cockpit of a plane, but I knew from my father—who was big, but not nearly as big as Jim—that it was a very tight fit for him. Could Jim even be a pilot? But wait, there were other planes ... Surely he'd fit in the cockpit of a Lancaster or another big bomber. Any plane that could carry twenty thousand pounds of bombs could certainly carry Jim.

We entered another room and immediately joined the back of another line. At the front of this line were four or five women—the first women I'd seen here—dressed in white nurse's uniforms, and they were giving the inoculations. Each man stopped in front of each woman and received a shot in his left arm.

At first it didn't look too bad, but the closer I got, the more I could see, and hear, the reactions. The men were trying to be brave, maybe especially because they were standing there with the other recruits and in front of a group of women, but I could see their pained looks, and some of them jerked or even yelped a little bit. Of course, anybody who reacted that way was instantly razzed by the guys standing around him.

I was going to work hard not to react even if I had to bite the inside of my cheek to stop myself. I'd been smaller than everybody else my whole life, and I'd learned that meant I had to be just about the bravest, the one who complained the least.

Getting closer, I felt the sweat start to drip down my sides. At least it was where nobody could see it. I brushed my hand against my forehead just to make sure there was no sweat running down my face.

"Roll up your sleeves!" a corporal yelled.

Why was everything yelled here—did they think we were all deaf?

"If you're right-handed, roll up your left sleeve to get the shots!" he called out. "If you're left-handed ... well, you should be able to figure that out yourself!"

I rolled up my sleeve and sidestepped until I was standing directly in front of the first nurse. Without exchanging so much as a word or losing a second, she pulled out an enormous needle and jabbed me in the arm! I felt the pain shoot up my arm and into my head, and I grimaced—but nothing more.

"You only get one from me," the nurse said. "Keep moving."

"Yes, ma'am," I said as I moved sideways.

"You'd better not be calling *me* ma'am," the second nurse said.

I glanced up. She looked as though she wasn't much older than me! She gave me a wonderful smile.

"Then what should I call you?" I asked.

"Nurse Johnson," she said, sounding very formal, but her smile got even bigger.

"Hello, Nurse Johnson. I'm ready for my shot."

She was holding a hypodermic needle in her hand. She was ready too. I turned slightly to reveal my shoulder and she leaned across the counter and placed a hand against my arm, lifting it up.

"This isn't going to hurt at all."

"I bet you say that to all the guys."

"Just the ones I like."

I looked away from the needle and up into her eyes. Even her eyes were smiling and friendly. I felt a little pinch and some pressure, but no pain.

"There, was that so bad?"

"It's over?"

"I told you it wasn't going to hurt. Didn't you believe me?"

"Yeah, sure, I guess."

"It's not very gentlemanly to question the word of a lady," she joked.

"I wasn't—"

"Move it along, this isn't a date!"

I spun around. The sergeant was standing right behind me, so close I could feel his hot breath against my face.

"Yes, Sergeant!" I yelled back. I offered an awkward salute, and as I brought my arm up, I realized that it was already hurting where I'd gotten the first shot.

"No salute, remember—I work for a living!"

I quickly moved over to the third nurse. She was neither young nor friendly looking. She actually looked like somebody who wasn't going to care if the shot hurt or not. She pressed the needle against my arm and slipped the end in. There was nothing but a little pinch—even less than Nurse Johnson's.

"That was really good," I said.

"Some things get better with experience," she replied. "But don't think that means I'm going to be dating you, either."

I burst into laughter along with everybody else—including the sergeant!

"We got ourselves a lover boy here!" the sergeant bellowed. "Don't let his age fool you, gentlemen. You'd better lock up your wives, daughters, and mothers!"

"And which one of those do you think I am?" the nurse demanded, faking annoyance.

"I'd be proud if you were any of those to me, but I think wife would fit the best," he said, bowing gracefully from the waist.

"You are a charmer, Wilbur," she said.

"Wilbur?" Johnnie, who was standing just over from me, said loud enough for everybody, including the sergeant, to hear.

"You think that's funny?" the sergeant said as he stuck his finger into Johnnie's face.

"No ... of course ... of course not," he stammered.

"Don't you mean no, *Sergeant?*" he bellowed.

"Yes, Sergeant!"

"Or do you think you should be calling me by my first name?" he demanded.

"No, Sergeant!" he replied.

The sergeant—Wilbur—mumbled a few more words under his breath and walked away, shaking his head.

Johnnie looked over at me and Jim. "I really got to learn to keep my mouth shut."

Again everybody laughed. The sergeant glanced over his shoulder, and for a split second I thought he was going to come back, but he kept walking.

"You might be the first aircraftman who washes out before he has a chance to put on his uniform," Jim said to him.

Johnnie opened his mouth to say something and then thought better of it. He closed his mouth, mimed turning a key to seal his lips, and then pretended to put the key in his pocket. Almost at the same instant the fifth nurse jabbed him with a needle. Unprepared, he let out a little scream and jumped off the ground, which triggered more laughter.

The fifth needle went into my arm and the fifth set of initials was recorded. I was now officially inoculated. Once I was trained to fly, I could be sent overseas.

"I didn't know you were such a ladies' man," Jim said.

"You know what they say: good things come in small packages."

"They also say you can't get too much of a good thing."

I looked back at Nurse Johnson. She was certainly very pretty. She had such a nice smile and beautiful eyes and ... she was batting them at the next recruit in line, and laughing, and she took his arm and leaned in close as she gave him his shot. I watched her then do the same thing to the next aircraftman in line. Either she flirted with everybody or this was just her favourite technique for giving somebody a shot.

"Let's keep moving," Jim said, giving me a little push forward.

I willingly complied. I was just grateful he hadn't noticed her flirting with anybody else. Being thought of as a ladies' man wasn't the worst reputation to start off with. It sure beat the heck out of being made fun of for my size.

Up ahead was a door with a large red cross and the word MEDIC written in block letters. I looked down at my list. I was suddenly afraid we were going to get more shots behind that door. I was relieved to see on the sheet that it was only a physical and an eye exam.

I opened the door and froze in place. Standing in front of me were a bunch of naked men in two rows!

5

Jim bumped into me from behind, knocking me forward. I turned around. His expression showed he was as surprised as I was. Had we wandered into the wrong place, or—

"Remove your clothing and place it with your newly issued uniforms in the back cubbyholes!" a corporal yelled. "Then assemble in rows for your physical examination!"

Both of us, as well as Johnnie and a couple of other guys, walked toward where the corporal was pointing. Men were already there, some undressing and others, who I assumed had finished their examinations, getting re-dressed, but this time in their uniforms!

I picked out a cubby at the end of the row, a few away from anybody else. This was not feeling very comfortable at all.

I placed my uniform in the cubby and then sat down on the bench and pulled off my shoes, not bothering to untie them. Next came my shirt and pants. I was so grateful that I had on new underwear. I stood up and wiggled out of them, placing them on top of my other clothing.

I felt a sudden rush of embarrassment. Where was I supposed to look? Where was I supposed to put my hands? Jim was already walking toward the back rank. I didn't want to lose him, so I took my list, put my head down, and started walking.

A corporal appeared right in front of me. There was a confused look on his face. "Acey-deucey, are you afraid of catching a cold?"

"What, Corporal?" I asked.

He pointed down. I was still wearing my socks! I lifted my leg, reached down, and grabbed one, pulling it off, and then the second, while hopping, almost stumbling, but still keeping my balance. I tossed them back at my cubbyhole and they both went in!

I joined a row of six men, Jim on one side of me, Johnnie on the other. In front of us was another row of equally naked men standing at ease—although I didn't imagine anybody was feeling much ease or comfort.

Standing there in the buff, on the concrete floor, with a breeze blowing in through the windows at the top of the walls, I wished I could have kept my socks on. I shifted slightly from foot to foot, which I noticed other people were doing as well. I had to fight the urge to hold the sheet of paper with my list directly in front of me in a vain attempt at a little bit of privacy and dignity.

There was no conversation, and as I risked a glance around, I saw that everybody else was staring at the ground in front of them. I obviously wasn't the only person finding this less than comfortable.

A man—equally naked—came through a door at the front. It opened from a small cubicle, and inside was a man wearing a laboratory coat. I guessed that was the doctor.

A man in the first row was called forward and ushered through the door. The aircraftman in the second row stepped forward to take his place. There were three other doors, and I watched as men moved in and out of those as well, until finally it was my turn.

I walked into the little cubicle, nervous, but grateful not to be standing out in the big room any longer.

"Name?" the doctor asked as he took my list from me.

"McWilliams ... David, *sir*."

I liked the fact that the last name was always said first in the military. McWilliams *was* my last name and I wasn't going to stumble over that. But I was worried that I might accidentally blurt out Robert or Robbie instead of David.

"Do you have any medical conditions?" the doctor asked.

"No, sir."

"Are you on any medications, do you have any allergies, or have you had any medical operations?"

"No, sir, to all of those."

As he was asking the questions, he was looking in my ears with a light and poking me in my gut and sides with his fingers. I assumed he wasn't doing that just to irritate me or amuse himself.

He took the stethoscope that was around his neck, placed the ends in his ears, and started listening to my heart. Well, at least that's what I figured he was doing, because he was moving it all over my chest area. He circled around and started to tap me on the back and sides.

"Okay, son, you've passed your physical," he said, and he handed me back my sheet, with a dozen new sets of initials on it.

"Thank you, sir."

I walked back into the waiting area, where fifteen or twenty pairs of eyes glanced up and then returned their gaze to the floor again. I made my way back to the cubbies, and I can honestly say that I'd never been so grateful to be pulling on my underwear. I reached for the rest of my clothing and then stopped. I wasn't supposed to be putting on my clothing—I was supposed to be getting into my new uniform!

I slipped on the pants. Bluish-tinged wool—the colour of the air force. It was rough to the skin, but it felt good to put them on. It wasn't just about being allowed to get dressed at last; it was about *what* I was getting dressed in. This was the beginning of my new life. Once I'd put on the uniform, I was no longer a seventeen-year-old kid escaping boarding school; I was an acey-deucey ... an aircraftman second class.

"Hurry up! People are waiting for your spot!" the corporal screamed, and I jumped back into action.

I pulled on the shirt and buttoned it up, then I pulled on the pants. They were a bit loose, which I figured was better than too tight. I followed up with the socks. I stood up. The pants were a bit long, the cuffs dragging on the ground, but once I put on the boots, I figured they'd be fine. I slipped my foot into the first boot. It was a bit tighter than I would have liked, but it fit. I did the same with the second boot and then tied the laces.

Now for the final touch. I took the wedge cap and placed it on my head. I adjusted it, trying to find a comfortable place where it would fit and sit.

"Here, let me help you," Jim said.

I hadn't even noticed him there. He was dressed—
although his pants ended a good two inches above the tops
of his boots. I thought about asking him if he was expecting
a flood, but I decided I was the last person in the world to
bother anybody about their height.

He took the cap and adjusted it so it was sitting more off
to the side of my head.

"That does it. Now you look like a proper acey-deucey.
You might even want to go back to see that nurse. You know
what they say: women love a man in uniform."

"Maybe later. What's next on the list?"

"Eye examination. I've never been one for school, but
that's one examination I'm pretty sure I can pass."

Jim asked a corporal for directions, and we hurried
away only to once again find ourselves at the back of
a long line. This was really starting to become a pattern.
As we waited, there was a lot of good-natured conversation, laughter, and jokes. Everybody looked pretty
proud of their new uniforms, and it seemed as though we
were all standing just a little bit straighter, a little taller—
even me.

I shuffled forward with the line as one by one each man
had his eye exam, until it was my turn, right after Jim. I
handed my sheet over to the corporal in charge.

"Close your left eye," he said, "and use your right eye. Can you read the third line?"

"Sure. L ... E ... F ... O ... D—"

"Are you blind, son?" he demanded. "That's not the third row."

"Sure it is ... Oh, wait, do you mean the third from the top or the bottom?"

"The top."

"Sorry, I was counting up from the bottom. Do you want me to read the bigger letters first?"

"Forget it. You only needed the seventh row and that's the eleventh. Can you do the same with your other eye?"

I read the letters out easily. "Do you want me to do the bottom line as well? I can do it if you want."

"No need to test your eyes any further. You've got the eyes of an eagle."

I wanted to tell him that was what a pilot needed, but I stayed quiet as he handed me back my list, complete with more initialled spaces.

"Thank you, Corporal."

I joined Jim, who was waiting at the door.

"Next up is grooming," he said.

"Grooming? What does that mean?"

Jim removed my cap and ran his hand over my scalp,

making a buzzing sound, and suddenly I got it: we were going to have our hair buzzed off! I guessed that wasn't the worst thing. But then again, if I couldn't grow a moustache to change my appearance and look older, I wasn't sure that cutting off my hair would help much either. I'd still look young, but now with no hair.

I turned over on my side and my arm screamed out a reminder of the injections. I shifted again to relieve the pain and make my arm go back to simply feeling numb. Then I sat up in bed and slowly brought my deadened arm, which felt like a piece of lead, up to my head to run my hand over the stubble where my hair used to be. Gone were the long locks, and all that was left was prickly to the touch. At least my cap fit better now.

All around me in the darkness were hundreds and hundreds of men. Judging from the snoring, most of them were sound asleep. I was tired—no, I was exhausted—but I couldn't seem to drift off. It had been such a long day, such a different day, from the injections to the medicals, the issuing of the uniforms and the "housewife."

What a disappointment to learn that a housewife was only a box containing polish for our boots as well as buttons, needles and thread, and other things we'd need to keep our kits spic and span. I'd already put mine to good use. Before we turned in, Jim had let down the cuffs of his pants, giving him another inch of material, and I'd taken mine up so they wouldn't drag along the ground.

I couldn't help thinking that my mother would be pretty amused if she heard about me fixing my own pants like that. Then, strangely, I thought about what that would look like in a letter home.

Hello Mom, just wanted to tell you about fixing the trousers of my air force uniform … Oh, by the way, I've run away from boarding school and am now in the air force … Say hello to everybody at home … Lots of love … Your son who was called Robert but now is known as David.

Maybe I was getting a little punch-drunk from not having slept. I rolled over on my side, my left arm to the top this time, and tried to think of something that would help me get to sleep. My mind's eye focused on that nurse—Nurse Johnson. She was very pretty, and even if she did flirt with half the men on the base, I was still part of the half she flirted with. I wondered what her first name was. Probably something pretty. Maybe I'd even find out.

October 1, 1943

Dear Chip,

First off, I apologize for the delay in writing. I had planned to write to you much sooner, but I have found myself so exhausted every night that I've been too tired to put pen to paper. Some evenings I've been too tired to even pick up a pen, let alone have the mental capacity to put words together in a manner that approaches normal grammar and spelling. But enough of my sorry excuses. Having spent years in school and hearing a variety of your oh-so-clever reasons for not completing assignments, I must bow before the master.

After you receive this letter, I would like you to mail off the first letter to my mother. PLEASE, make sure it is letter number one. She would be rather confused to receive the second letter, in which I detail the party for All Saints' night and the Hallowe'en costume I wore.

She would be most shocked, I imagine, to see the costume I actually am wearing—my air force uniform. I would also imagine that there is a good chance she wouldn't recognize me. Not only have I lost all my hair to a very close buzz cut, but I've managed to gain ten pounds during the past four weeks. I do believe I could walk right past her—or you—and she wouldn't even recognize me.

My weight gain is rather shocking since our daily regimen involves morning calisthenics, a regular five-mile run, a strong belief that we should always run about at double time, and a diet of chores that includes kitchen duty, mopping floors, and keeping the grounds well tended. They have a saying here: "If it's on the ground, pick it up. If you can't pick it up, paint it. If you can't paint it, salute it." I do a great deal of saluting. My rank—aircraftman second class—means that everything and everybody is superior to me, and they waste little time in pointing that out to us.

I have never walked—or, more precisely, marched—so much in my life. I had no idea that flying a plane and fighting Hitler would involve drills. Over and over we practise until thirty or more of us can move, turn, and stop in unison. I feel more like I've joined a dance company than the military. I think the plan is that if we're ever shot down over occupied Europe, we can march all the way to Berlin in a precise military manner. Then, upon our arrival, Adolf will be so impressed with our drills that he will admit the inferiority of his so-called Master Race and simply surrender.

I hope school is going well for you. With my absence, I would suppose that Headmaster Beamish no longer needs to divide his time between us and is focusing his great insights and wisdom more directly on you. What a delight that must be. I hope you have been keeping your nose clean and staying out of trouble— while still initiating enough mischief to keep yourself confined to the dungeon (a.k.a. the mailroom).

I mistakenly thought that by enlisting I could escape the drudgery of school work that I had left behind. That has not been the case. While you slack off or fall asleep during class, I am compelled to not only go to class but pay full attention! Some things, such as studying the parts of an airplane, the physics behind flight, and regulations seem to make sense and are fascinating. Other areas, such as history and mathematics, are just as boring as they were when I was sitting beside you. The only difference is that I dare not drift off or I'll have a corporal or sergeant bellowing in my ear. Apparently, becoming a non-com (that's short for "non-commissioned officer") involves losing the ability to speak in a normal voice. All corporals and sergeants yell at all times. I can only picture what life must be like for their poor wives!

For what it's worth, I have scored extremely high in all aspects of mathematics, and the staff sergeant who is the instructor says I have "a knack" for finding my way around a map. I think that might come in handy—I would imagine that it's always best for a pilot to be able to find his way both to the target and back home at the end.

For the privilege of working like a dog, I am rewarded with the princely sum of $1.10 each day. For me, with nobody to support and nothing really to spend it on, this goes a long way. For others, especially those who have a wife and children to support back home, or an "itch to scratch," be it booze or cigarettes or gambling, the money doesn't go far.

Technically it is illegal to drink on duty or while on the base, but it often seems easier to find hooch than water. As for smoking, there are far fewer of us who have no use for the weed than those who smoke. I still regard it as a rather filthy habit, and I am unsure how some of these men—who can't seem to go more than an hour or so without a ciggie—will manage during a long flight. Do they plan on stepping out onto the wing for a puff?

I am also writing to inform you that my time here at Manning is at an end. These four weeks have passed ... as have I! I am being transferred to a flight school! I am, according to military censorship rules, unable to tell you exactly where I am going, but the postmark on my next letter will probably give you a good idea of my destination.

A number of men who have become my friends are coming along with me. Closest are Jim, whom I met on the train ride, and Johnnie. Jim is a big farm boy who has nothing but good words for everybody he meets—although I wouldn't want to be the one to get him mad. Johnnie reminds me of you. He's finally——after numerous punishment details on KP peeling potatoes—learning to keep his mouth shut. Still he's bloody good entertainment, and it's always interesting to see what new trouble he's going to find himself in. As I said, he does remind me very much of you.

I had better be signing off. Best wishes to you and your family, and my thanks for all your help.

With fondness,
Davie

7

"Does anybody care to make a small wager on who might have scored the highest in our latest examination?" the instructor asked as he held the tests up in his right hand.

"Can I put my money on McWilliams?" Johnnie asked.

The instructor cocked his head to the side. "Don't you have enough faith to want to bet on yourself?"

"I haven't been to church enough in my life to have *that* much faith," Johnnie replied, and a roar of laughter erupted.

"Settle down, everybody. The last thing we want to do is encourage him. He is right, though. Top marks on our orientation quiz go to McWilliams. Let's give him a hand."

The boys started to clap and cheer and whistle. Jim leaned over and gave me a slap on the back.

Our instructor put the paper down on my desk. A big fifty out of fifty was marked in red pen at the top right corner. "Not only did he have top marks, he had perfect marks!"

Again there was a round of cheers.

"As for the rest of you," he said as he continued to hand out the papers, "there were some good marks, some passable marks, and some who did so poorly in understanding the concepts of orientation that I am surprised they were even able to find their way into this room to take the test in the first place!"

I looked over at Jim as he received his paper. He looked at it, nodded his head, and turned it so I could see the mark: 32/50. Navigation—and mathematics in general—wasn't his strength, but he made up for it by studying hard.

"You have now been here two and a half weeks," the instructor said. "Today is the halfway point in your time at the Initial Training School. While some, like McWilliams here, have taken full advantage of the time and training, others have been less, shall we say, dedicated. You may have noticed the empty chairs in the room today."

I *had* noticed, and wondered if there was a touch of the flu going around—or maybe the kind of flu that came in a bottle the morning after a night of drinking. A few of the guys always indulged way too much.

"Those empty seats belong to those members of your class who have washed out of the program."

Everybody now did a serious scan of the room, trying to figure out who was still there and who was gone. Instantly I picked up a couple of the missing faces, because I'd already figured out who was on the edge. Everyone who had passed basic training at Manning—and that was almost everybody—had made the trip to flight school together. We'd left Manitoba behind and were now in Saskatchewan, stationed outside Regina. But the training was getting harder—especially all the math—and it looked as though they were whittling our numbers down already.

"Some of those men might yet become ground crew. Others simply do not have what it takes and have been asked to consider enlisting in something that requires less ability ... perhaps army or navy."

There were derisive hoots from the back of the room. We all knew which branch of the military was the best—although I wasn't about to mention that to any sailors or soldiers unless we clearly outnumbered them.

"That does not mean that those of you who remain are in the clear," the instructor pointed out. "Some of you are hanging on by the skin of your teeth."

I wasn't certain, but I thought he glanced at Johnnie. Johnnie didn't seem to notice.

"Does anybody care to venture a guess as to why some of you are doing better in your studies than others?" he asked.

"McWilliams hasn't been out of high school that long, so he's used to taking tests?" one of the men suggested.

"McWilliams looks like he should still *be* in high school," the instructor replied. "But some of you have recently graduated from university and are not doing as well. Which, I might say, tells us something about the quality of our institutions of higher learning." He paused. "Since no answer is forthcoming, I'm going to provide it myself. The difference is that while some students are here studying, doing additional reading, and peppering their instructors with extra questions, some of you are drinking, gambling, and sneaking out to carouse and get into fist fights."

This time he did look directly at Johnnie. Johnnie was sporting an only slightly faded black eye. He'd told the commanding officer he'd received it falling on a wet floor. I didn't think the CO—or anybody else for that matter—believed him, but they couldn't prove anything different, especially since half a dozen guys claimed to have "witnessed" the event.

Technically, we were allowed out on leave only on Saturday nights, but that hadn't stopped some of the guys from sneaking off base for a little excitement. Last Thursday six or seven of the guys, including Johnnie, had climbed out of a window after lights out, *borrowed* a truck, and gone down to the Hotel Saskatchewan in downtown Regina.

Apparently the male population of Regina didn't think too much of the fly boys in training. Maybe women liked a man in uniform, but the local men didn't feel the same way. Farmers were classified as essential workers—they were needed to work on the home front to avoid food short-ages—but some of them were pretty touchy about the fact that they hadn't been able to join up, and they didn't take kindly to the guys in uniform coming in and flirting with their lady folk. I'd seen a few of them around the town and they were big, strong-looking guys. And from what Johnnie told me, when the locals and the fly boys mixed it up, there were some cuts and bruises on both sides, but the fly boys got the worst of it. Johnnie had been in more than a few of these dust-ups. At least he'd been able to get away before the military police showed up, and he'd always made it back to base without being caught ... so far.

"If any of you feel that your training here is getting in the way of your social life, you will not succeed. You might as well grab a rifle and join the army. And as you slog through the mud, sleep in foxholes, and eat army grub, I want you to look up in the sky as our planes fly overhead."

He pointed up as if he were really watching a plane fly by, and we all looked up as if we could see the plane he was imagining. In my head, though, I *could* see it.

Obviously, it was a Spitfire, and just as obviously, I was in the cockpit.

"And when you see that plane, remember what *could* have been … if you had been prepared to work." He chuckled to himself. "You are all now to report to the Link Trainer."

There were a few cheers from the men.

"For some of you, this is the closest you'll ever get to flying," the instructor said. "Scoring well on tests is necessary, but not enough. If you can't fly the simulator, you won't be getting the chance to fly the real thing. *Dismissed!*"

We gathered in a semicircle around the trainer. In front of us was such a strange little contraption. With its stubby little wings and lack of propeller, it looked more like a cartoon drawing of a plane than a real one. And of course, it wasn't a real plane. It was a flight simulator.

"Good afternoon, gentlemen," the sergeant began. "This is, of course, the Link Trainer, a flight simulator named after its inventor, Edwin Link. He saw the folly in putting raw recruits up in real airplanes. Up there," he said, pointing to the sky, "a mistake most often translates into three things: a lost plane, a dead instructor, and a dead recruit. Instructors and aircraft are far too valuable to waste."

He didn't mention the recruit, which of course said what he really thought about wasting one of us—not a great loss.

"And that is why we would never dream of actually allowing any of you at this stage to fly a *real* plane. But in this flight simulator, down here, a mistake means nothing."

That was easy for him to say. A mistake or two down here would translate into washing out as a pilot. I knew that. I also knew that all the work I'd been putting into learning the physics of flight wouldn't mean anything if I couldn't actually fly.

"While it certainly looks different on the outside, the controls on this simulator—the yoke, the rudders, and the control panel—are almost identical to those used in actual aircraft. Having flown both Harvards and Gypsy Moths, the two most common training aircraft some of you will eventually be allowed to fly, I can tell you that this handles in a very similar way."

All the training aircraft were painted bright yellow to make them more visible in the sky—and on the ground if they crashed. There was no need for them to be camouflaged to blend into the sky because there was no enemy there to hide from.

"This trainer uses a complicated series of pumps and

valves to simulate real flight. When you pull back on the yoke, it will climb. When you push it forward, it will descend. The floor pedals do control the rudders, and in conjunction with the ailerons, you can turn and bank as you would in a real plane. There is nothing, I repeat, *nothing* in this cockpit that you have not been taught, studied, and been tested on. If you did well on your tests, you technically know how to fly a plane."

I felt reassured. I'd done well on all the tests—top of the class in virtually everything—and understood not just the controls but the physics and laws of aerodynamics that allowed flight to happen. I knew that a skid would happen if I used too much rudder and not enough ailerons. I knew a sideslip would take place if I banked too hard and too fast. I knew the minimum airspeed that had to be maintained to avoid a stall. I knew the techniques inside and out. I guess the next question was whether or not I could put them into practice.

"There is, however, one significant flaw with this and any other simulator," the sergeant said. "Up in the sky, it's just you and your instructor, or perhaps just you. Those minor mistakes you make are just between the two of you, or you and God. Down here, with your entire class standing and watching and with your instructor bellowing out orders, everybody knows everything you do wrong. Now, do we have a volunteer to start?"

Hands went up all around me. I wanted to try it, but I was in no rush to be the very first person to—

"McWilliams, do I see your hand up?" he asked.

I startled in response. "No, Sergeant."

"Don't you want to become a pilot, son?"

"Yes, Sergeant."

"In that case, I think it's time that you got into a cockpit and took the yoke. After all, being good with a pencil and paper doesn't mean you're going to be good in the air. McWilliams, you're our first *volunteer*."

The military had the strangest definition of "volunteer." Reluctantly I stepped forward and was offered words of encouragement and a couple of pats on the back. Carefully placing one foot on the stubby little wing, I lifted the other over the side and stepped into the cockpit. I held on to both sides, slipped in and onto the seat. I was in the cockpit of a plane ... well, the fake cockpit of a fake plane, but at least it was a step in the right direction.

The cockpit was surprisingly large for such a little plane— not really spacious, but big enough for me. I wondered, though, how it would be for Jim with his long legs. I put my hands on the yoke. Gently, carefully, I pulled it forward and then pushed it away. It glided effortlessly. Next I moved my feet, making sure they were on the two rudder pedals. I pushed first the left and then the right, and they responded.

"Turn the trainer on!" the instructor bellowed.

The machine began to hum. It jerked a little and then rose a foot or so higher as the valves filled with air. The dials also came to life. There were a lot of dials. I knew that, and I knew what they were for, but still I felt a mounting sense of panic. I could feel sweat starting to roll down my sides.

"Okay, McWilliams, you're live. Take control of the aircraft!" he yelled.

Slowly I pulled the yoke toward me and the nose of the plane rose up, the pitch increasing as I continued to pull back. I glanced over my shoulder and saw the elevators—the little flaps on the back wing—respond the way they would on a real aircraft, rising up.

"Level it off!" he called out.

I pushed the yoke back and the pitch decreased until I was "flying" level. So far, this had been pretty easy.

"I want you to bank left!"

I depressed the left pedal—left rudder—and at the same time turned the yoke slightly to the left, causing the left aileron to drop and the right one to rise. The simulator dipped to the side as if I really were turning the plane!

"Harder bank! Tighter turn!" he yelled.

I pushed harder on the pedal, more rudder.

"Watch your yaw!" the instructor bellowed. "You're starting to skid!"

Right, I was applying too much rudder and not using enough aileron! I gave it more and the little plane banked harder. It tilted even farther until my left side was pressed against the wall of the cockpit.

"Good, good, now level it out!" he called.

Slowly I did the opposite of what I'd done to get into the bank. I pushed down on the right pedal to create right rudder and turned the yoke to the right, this time doing it harder to try to avoid a skid in the other direction, and the plane responded.

"Watch your pitch!" he yelled.

In turning the yoke, I'd pulled it toward me as well, and I hadn't noticed that I'd started to climb. I pushed it back a few degrees and felt the difference as the nose dipped.

"Climbing while turning can produce a stall if you don't increase the throttle at the same time!" the instructor called out.

I hadn't even thought about the throttle or the airspeed. I looked down and around. The throttle was just off to the right, and beside it was my airspeed indicator. Apparently I was flying at just under 180 miles per hour.

"Time to bring her in for a landing," he called out.

I was already running level—no pitch, no yaw, and no bank. I slowly pushed the yoke forward, and the front end of the plane tilted downward the way it was supposed to. This was all going very well.

"Enemy aircraft coming up behind you at five o'clock!" the instructor screamed as loudly as he could. "Take evasive action, quick, quick, quick!"

I pushed down hard on the right pedal and cranked the wheel to the right, while at the same time pushing the yoke forward to dive and pick up airspeed to escape! The little plane rocked and banked violently to the right as it responded to the controls.

"Well, that does it!" the instructor said. "Turn it off!"

There was a pause, and then the simulator hissed and sagged and levelled itself off, no longer responding to my attempts to control it. I reluctantly let go of the yoke. It had felt good in my hands.

"Let's give McWilliams a little round of applause!"

I climbed out, feeling elated and embarrassed.

"That was a very successful flight," he said. "At least until he crashed the plane."

I *what*? I turned to him, looking for an explanation.

"Did you think to look at the altimeter at any time during that flight?" he asked loudly.

I hadn't. I'd been so busy with the other controls that I hadn't even looked for it!

"When you decided to avoid that enemy attack by diving, you were certainly able to gain airspeed ... at least until you slammed into the ground. You started that dive at less than three hundred feet. That would have been a superb move at three or four thousand feet. Now, who's next?"

I climbed off the wing and dropped down to the ground as others raised their hands, each wanting his turn at the controls.

"You did well," Jim said to me under his breath.

"I crashed."

"Of course you crashed. He wasn't going to let you land without crashing, no matter what you did," he whispered.

"Do you really think so?"

"He wanted to make you an example. The next time will be different. You'll see."

"I hope so ... And thanks."

8

I sat on my bunk, my back against the wall, holding a flight instruction manual workbook. To anybody watching, and there were a couple dozen of the guys all around, it looked as though I was studying. But behind the manual, hidden from prying eyes, was the pad I was going to use to write a letter to my mother.

It wasn't like I was ashamed or embarrassed to be writing to her; people wrote letters home all time. It was just that if anybody saw the letter, I wouldn't be able to explain why I was writing about things that were happening at my boarding school.

These letters were necessary, but not necessarily easy. I felt bad lying to Mom, which seemed strange since my entire life these days was nothing but one big lie that I was keeping from her. Somehow, though, it seemed worse when I had to put it all down in writing. But there was no choice: in order to keep the big lie away from her, I had to keep up all the little ones.

October 15, 1943

Dear Mumsy,

I'd like to start off by apologizing for how short this letter is going to be. I'm neck-deep in work, and you'll be happy to know that I'm taking my studies more seriously than I ever have in my entire life!

That certainly wasn't a lie. My teachers had always accused me of not "applying" myself. Nobody was saying that here.

My marks, particularly in all of the mathematics areas, have been top of the class. My instructors have been using me as an example to motivate the other students.

Again, I was just telling the truth. My marks were also tops in navigation, orientation, and general aircraft flight dynamics, but I wasn't about to tell her that or try to explain it.

Given my newly discovered aptitude with numbers, I'm beginning to think that I might want to pursue accountancy, or something in the financial field, at university. Perhaps I could become a banker. Never bad to be around money!

As well, while I wasn't truly thinking much about accounting, I was starting to figure out an excuse for why I wouldn't be coming home in June.

If my mathematics marks continue at this level, I've been assured that I can enrol directly in an accounting class upon graduation this year. I know that it would mean not coming home for the summer, but I have been given reason to believe that I might even warrant a full scholarship for the program! That would simply be too good an opportunity to pass up, and it would help prepare me for university!

"Anybody for a little craps?" Johnnie asked.

I looked up, surprised to see him standing there. I'd been so lost in the letter that I hadn't noticed him coming. He was shaking a pair of dice in his left hand.

"I think I'll pass," I said.

"You can't still be studying," he said, shaking his head, a look of utter disgust on his face.

"I want to know where everything is the next time I get into the trainer, so I can be a better pilot."

"Didn't you see me up there?" he said. "I was the class ace."

"You were pretty good," I admitted.

It had been reassuring to me to watch as the instructor forced recruit after recruit to crash the simulator. After the third or fourth crash, it became clear that he wasn't letting anybody get out alive the first time. Clearly his greatest worry wasn't that we'd lose confidence but that we'd be too cocky.

Some had crashed almost immediately, while he'd had to work hard to make some of the others burst into flames. One of the hardest was Johnnie. Somehow his lack of interest in the classroom, theoretical part of flight hadn't hindered him in his handling of the simulator. We'd heard instructors talk about "natural pilots," and I was beginning to think that Johnnie was one of those—assuming he didn't wash out tomorrow by flunking another test or getting caught coming back in through the barracks window at four in the morning.

"And do you know the reason why I was so good?" Johnnie boasted.

"I was thinking blind, dumb luck?" Jim said. He got up from the lower bunk, where he'd been lying down, and the whole bed shook.

"I wouldn't rule that out completely," Johnnie replied. "But I think it has to do with all the craps I play."

"What?" I said.

"I gotta hear this," Jim said. "Explain."

"Well, if you think about it, flying is all about hand-to-eye coordination. And in shooting craps, everything depends on coordination in the wrist movement." He shook the dice in his hand and then mimed throwing them.

Jim and I cracked up at that, but it didn't seem to bother Johnnie at all, because he had a grin a mile wide.

"That's priceless, Johnnie. Next you'll be telling us that having a good belt of whisky makes you a better pilot too," Jim taunted him.

"Maybe it does. Good pilots are relaxed pilots, and maybe a shot or two relaxes me."

"And chasing the local ladies? Are you going to explain how that makes you better at flying?"

"That one's easy. My pursuit of the honeys has resulted in me having to take evasive action on more than one occasion." He paused and pointed to his eye. "Not to mention that it's given me combat experience!"

Both Jim and I—and everyone else listening to Johnnie's routine—broke into laughter again.

"You're wasting your time becoming a pilot," Jim said. "You should be on the radio with Jack Benny and the other comedians."

"I guess there'd be more money in that, but I'm in this

for King and Country. At the rate I'm training, and with all these sacrifices I'm making to become a good pilot, I might become the greatest Canadian air ace since Billy Bishop!" he trumpeted, and there was even more laughter. "Well, how else can you explain it? You certainly can't think it comes from any book!" Johnnie exclaimed.

Before I could react, he reached up and snatched my book, letter and all, out of my hands. The book he took away, but the letter fluttered to the ground.

"Give me that!" I screamed.

Before I could even think to react, he grabbed the letter from the ground. "Let's see who Davie here is writing to! Maybe the ladies' man has got himself a girlfriend!" he said as he danced away.

I jumped down to the ground and tried to take the letter, but he fended me off with one arm and started to read.

"'Dear Mumsy' ... Mumsy? ... Shoot, he's writing to his *mother*."

Before Johnnie could get any further, Jim reached over and swiped the letter back and handed it to me. Thank goodness.

"Might as well let him have his letter back," Jim said, "especially seeing as we're not sure you can actually read."

Johnnie just laughed. "Well, fellas, while you're wasting

your time writing letters and studying books," he said, slapping the workbook with his free hand, "I'm putting mine to good use to become a better pilot, according to my own patented training system. Now, are you interested in playing, yes or no?"

"I'll pass. When I finish my letter, I'm going to study," I replied.

"I think I'll play some craps," Jim said. "He might just have something there. No other reason I can think of for him to be any good in the air."

"That's what I like to hear!" Johnnie chirped. He tossed the book to me and I caught it. "As for you, don't wear your eyes out studying, and send your mother our *love!*"

"Yeah, right."

I climbed back up onto my bunk. I smoothed out the paper, which had gotten a little crinkled in the exchange. The very bottom of the sheet had also been ripped. I thought about starting over, but that seemed like too much effort. It was best just to continue with this one.

Of course, with things going the way they are in the war, even though I'm eager to begin training as an accountant, university will probably have to wait a little longer.

There was no need to say any more, because we'd argued about it often enough. She also knew that by summer, she wouldn't be able to stop me from enlisting. Besides, I really couldn't let her sidetrack me. My only hope of all of this *never* being discovered was to continue to write to her from overseas next year, after telling her I'd enlisted on my eighteenth birthday. She wouldn't have to know that I'd really enlisted a whole eleven months earlier. And even though by then I'd be flying in combat, I'd just pretend that I was still in basic training. And on the bright side, she'd be less worried thinking I was still in training and not yet flying missions. So, in a strange way, I was lying to make it easier for her. That was how I had to think about it.

Back to the correspondence. A letter from Chip had arrived and it contained the sort of tidbits that would keep the boarding school illusion alive. Even better, his letter contained correspondence that my mother had sent to me at school, so I was able to work some realistic details into my letter to her.

I don't know if you had a bad storm last week, but we certainly had one in Toronto. A couple of trees on the school grounds were hit. One was split right down the middle as if it had been struck

by a giant with an axe. The lightning and thunder were so bad
that it practically shook me out of bed.

I was so sad to hear about Mrs. Henderson. She led a long
life and I know she'll be remembered fondly by all who knew her.
Please send on my condolences and my regrets at not being able
to attend the funeral.

I said a silent thanks to Chip.

He'd also written to tell me that he was slogging away
in school and getting the best marks of his life. Maybe what
our teachers had always said was right: we were a bad influ-
ence on each other. He also promised, though, that come
early December, he'd stir up enough to keep himself stuck
in the mailroom.

Please send my love to the girls, and even to Scotty (just
kidding, little brother). I miss you all and love you all very much.
Your loving son,

I stopped myself, in shock. I'd almost written *David*, the
first stroke already made. I could easily fix that. It would
have been so much easier just to write *McWilliams*.

Robbie.

There, that did it. Now I'd put the letter in an envelope, address it to my mother at my home address, and put it in a bigger envelope that I'd mail to Chip. Of course, I'd write him a letter as well. It was good to have one person in the world with whom I could be honest.

"McWilliams."

That startled me! It was a corporal standing beside my bunk.

"CO wants to see you in his office."

"He does? Do you know what it's about?"

He pointed at the two stripes on his shoulder. "I know you might find this hard to believe, but the commanding officer generally doesn't share his thoughts with me. I'm more his clerk than his best buddy."

"Oh, yeah, of course, sorry," I mumbled.

"But if you want, I'll just go back and ask him, you know, to make sure it's something important enough to make you want to come and see him … I'm sure he'll understand."

"That's okay," I said as I jumped down from my bunk.

I started off and suddenly remembered that my letter was sitting up there on the bed. What if it blew down or somebody picked it up and looked at it? I ran back and grabbed it, stuffing it in my pocket.

"He did say on the double, so I wouldn't keep him waiting if I were you!"

"No, Corporal!" I replied. I started off, running at what could only be called triple time.

9

As I ran to the CO's office, I started to get worried. Why would he want to see me? Had I done something wrong? Or worse, was he sending me home? I'd heard that every candidate who washed out had been personally informed by him, and— No, that was just crazy. I was doing better than anybody on the tests, and maybe I'd crashed the Link, but so had everybody else. There was no reason he'd be sending me—

Outside the office, I skidded to a stop. There *was* a reason. I'd been found out. It had to be that. He knew who I was— and who I *wasn't*. For the first two weeks at Manning that was all I'd thought about, but since then it had been nothing more than a passing idea. I just figured, if they hadn't found out yet, they weren't going to—unless, of course, my mother had somehow stumbled onto my plot and contacted the authorities.

I stood there, frozen in place, paralyzed by the thought that I'd been discovered. Part of me wanted to go back to the barracks, gather my stuff, and climb out the window that Johnnie always used for his escapes. But I knew that was even crazier. If I had been discovered, there was no place to run, and certainly no place to hide. And if I hadn't, there was no point in keeping the CO waiting.

The waiting area outside his office was empty. The corporal who had come to get me, his clerk, who usually sat at the desk outside the door, wasn't back yet, and the door to the inner office was closed. I thought about taking a seat and waiting until either the corporal returned or the door opened, but I was too anxious to sit there and stew.

I knocked on the door.

"Come!" came the reply from behind the door.

I opened it, stepped in, and saluted. "You wanted to see me, *sir*!"

He returned my salute. "At ease, McWilliams. Take a seat."

"Yes, sir!" I replied sharply, and sat down in the chair right in front of his desk.

"Cigarette?" he said, holding out a package with two cigarettes poking out.

"No, thank you, sir."

"Don't you smoke?" he asked.

"No, sir."

"Do you mind if I do?"

His question caught me by surprise. "No, of course not, sir."

"Good."

He flicked open a fancy silver lighter and lit his cigarette. He inhaled deeply and then let out a big puff of smoke.

"I've got to tell you, McWilliams, that I have a lot of respect for you men who don't waste any time in enlisting. Do you know you're the youngest man in the program?"

"Yes, sir, I thought I might be." Actually, since I was only seventeen, I was completely certain I was the youngest person who'd ever been through this training school.

"And despite that, your marks have been nothing short of excellent."

"I have good instructors, sir."

"Everybody here has the same instructors. Some people just have more of what it takes."

Obviously, I wasn't being washed out, nor had I been discovered. I could feel my shoulders relax, and I realized that they'd been somewhere up around my ears.

He picked up a manila file folder that was on his desk. "Your marks in all areas have been excellent ... radio transmission, friend-or-foe recognition, basic airmanship, regulations, weaponry, and the dynamics and physics of flight … all excellent."

"Thank you, sir. I've been working hard, sir."

"But in some areas they are even better than simply excellent. Your marks in mathematics, understanding of compass directions, navigation and orientation, and the use of maps have been, without exception, without error. You are not only the top student in your group of aircraftmen, you are, in fact, the highest-scoring trainee we have had in the four-year history of this program!"

I tried to stay formal and focused, but I couldn't stop myself from smiling. "I didn't know that, sir."

"I imagine you didn't. What you also didn't know was that the test you were administered yesterday for navigation was different from the one given to every other student in your program."

"It was? But why would … I mean no, sir, I didn't know that."

Come to think of it, it had seemed like a very hard test, and I'd wondered how the rest of the class had done.

"If I may ask, sir, why would my test be different?"

"The purpose of any test is to probe the ability of the person taking it. You are, no doubt, aware that you have received perfect marks on all examinations focused on mathematics, navigation, and orientation."

I did know that. I was proud of that.

"We felt that the tests designed to measure the achievement and knowledge expected of recruits at your level of experience and training were not gauging your true potential. So we decided to alter your test. Did you notice that the mathematical formulas necessary to determine navigational goals were omitted from your paper?"

"Yes, sir. I just assumed they were omitted from all tests, since it is important to have those formulas committed to memory."

"Most of the navigators now engaged in theatres of combat don't have those formulas memorized," he said. "They have cheat sheets to help them along."

"I figured in the heat of battle, it would be better to just know the formulas and how to apply them."

"And can you do that? Just write them down and apply them?"

"I can write them down, but I don't need to. I do the calculations in my head."

"You did the calculations for this test in your head?" he asked. He sounded very skeptical.

"Well ... yes ... yes, sir."

"Unbelievable," he muttered under his breath. "I want you to know that your instructor not only omitted those formulas, he also asked you to apply factors such as wind speed and payload weights. Were you surprised or confused by that?"

"A little surprised, sir, since we hadn't studied those things, but not confused."

"Why not?"

"I had done a little extra reading," I admitted. "But really, it's just common sense."

"It's far from common!" he exclaimed. "And we tested you further by asking you to plot your final destination through a multi-course route with mid-air corrections for an *exact* arrival time."

It had been a hard test. It was the first time I'd doubted myself, wondering if I had the right answers.

"Would you like to know how you did?"

I nodded.

"I have that test right here," he said, tapping his finger against a paper on his desk. He picked it up and handed it to me. Across the top in red pen it read 100/100!

"Those questions that you answered were taken directly from the final exams given to navigators before they are assigned to a flight crew, and you achieved a perfect score! That is an incredible accomplishment."

"Thank you, sir."

"Son, what you're accomplishing is very admirable, but not surprising."

He reached down and removed another piece of paper from the folder on his desk. I caught a glance and recognized the letter he was holding. It was the letter *I'd* written on school stationery, the one I'd given to Chip to mail for me from school.

"Your former headmaster, Mr. Beamish, described you in superlatives. He had nothing but praise for you, as a student and a person."

"That's good to hear, sir."

"He writes that you graduated at the top of your class, were student president, a class leader … Very commendable."

Maybe I had laid it on a bit thick. If he knew who wrote that letter, he'd have a very different opinion of me at this moment.

"He also mentioned that you want to be a pilot."

"Yes, sir."

"Your father was a pilot."

"My father *is* a pilot, sir."

He looked confused. "Wasn't he shot down ... He is a prisoner of war, isn't he?"

"Yes, sir, he was shot down and he is a prisoner of war, but he still is a pilot."

"Ah, yes ... of course ... I meant no offence," he apologized.

"No offence taken, sir."

"Your instructors have every confidence, and I agree, that you have the skills and aptitude to become a bomb aimer, a flight engineer, a pilot, or a navigator."

"I hope to become a pilot, sir."

"I know, son, following in the footsteps of your old man ... Very admirable. I think we all know that you could be a pilot."

"That's why I'm here, sir."

"And that's what makes this so hard for me to tell you." He paused and looked up at me. "Son, sometimes we don't necessarily get what we hope for."

My mouth dropped open. After all that he'd said, after all the work I'd done, somehow I was still being washed out! How was that possible?

"We know that you have the skills necessary to become a pilot," he went on. "In fact, *many* of the men who come here for training are capable of becoming pilots. But not many of them can become navigators. Navigators are the brains of the operation. You are being reassigned to navigator training."

"But I don't want to become a navigator!" I shouted out before I could stop myself. "I mean, sir, that I respectfully request that I be reconsidered to become a pilot."

"Son, it's our job not only to determine the path that is best for each recruit but, more importantly, to determine what is best for the air force. There is a desperate need for navigators."

"I thought pilots were in short supply too ... sir," I said.

"Pilots are ten for a penny. There are many men here in training who have the ability to become pilots, but very few would have the aptitude to become navigators, and quite frankly, I've never seen anybody with your ability. Because of that, you are being transferred directly to advanced training."

"Advanced training?"

"Yes. When we told them about your test score, they were only too happy to fast-track you. You must be happy about that."

"Yes, sir," I said, although I certainly didn't feel, look, or sound happy.

"Son, I know you're disappointed, but I want to be honest with you. I know that you could be a good pilot, but right now, at your age, nobody is going to give you that opportunity. You can't go into battle without the full confidence of your men. You're just too young to win the trust of the flight crew of a Lancaster."

"I don't want to fly a Lancaster. I want Spitfires."

He shook his head. "There wouldn't be much chance of that either. Spitfires are too valuable to give out to just anybody."

He got up from his seat, circled the desk, and sat down on the edge directly in front of me. He put a hand on my shoulder.

"Son, this isn't about what you want or what I want. If I had my way, I'd be over there flying missions. This is about what's needed to defeat the Nazis. We need you to become a navigator. Do you understand?"

I nodded my head. "Yes, sir ... I just know I could be a good pilot."

"I know you could too. I'm going to do something. I'm going to write a recommendation that upon the completion of your first tour of duty as a navigator, you be allowed to transfer to Elementary Flying Training School if you still wish to become a pilot."

"You'd do that?"

"Most certainly. And ten or so months from now, you'll be older and have gained more experience—experience that will serve you well. I'm going to put my recommendation in writing. I'll keep one copy on file, give you one to take with you, and send the third directly to the group captain where you'll be assigned."

"Where will I be assigned?"

"Somewhere in England."

"England!" I exclaimed.

"You'll be taking the train to Halifax, where you will board the *Queen Mary*, leaving port in four days' time."

My mouth dropped open.

"You'll be shipping out tomorrow, so you have tonight to pack your gear and say your goodbyes to your classmates." He paused. "And of course, since this is all so sudden, we'll allow you the opportunity to make a long-distance telephone call to inform your family of your reassignment."

"My family ... yes, that would be good," I mumbled.

"I'll have my clerk make that call right now. It would be an honour to speak to your mother and pass on my personal congratulations."

"Um ... that won't be possible ... We, uh ... we don't have a telephone at home," I stammered, trying madly to think of an excuse. "Money is tight, what with my father being gone. But there is an uncle I could call … my uncle Chip." Chip needed to know what was happening so the letters wouldn't come here again. "He's not really an uncle but a close, close friend of the family. I could call him … tomorrow … if that would be acceptable, sir."

"I'll make arrangements with my clerk for you to make that call first thing in the morning. You'll have to see the clerk tomorrow anyway. He has to make up your transfer papers and travel arrangements."

"Thank you, sir. I appreciate that, sir. I just think it would be better for my uncle to tell my mother … You know how mothers worry."

"I know how we all worry about our children. I'm glad my son is still too young to enlist, although he's only a year or so younger than you." He picked up a picture from his desk and handed it to me. "That's my wife, Betty, and our children—my daughter, Lorraine, who's twelve, and our son, Graham. He'll be seventeen on his next birthday."

He was basically my age, and he looked older than I did. I wondered when the picture was taken. I handed it back to him.

"My wife is entirely opposed to the idea of him enlisting. She says she doesn't want her baby going off to war. I tell her he isn't a baby, but truth be told, I'm not that crazy about it either." He looked up from the picture and directly at me. "How did your mother react when you told her you were joining the air force?"

"She wasn't too happy."

"I understand that. The very worst part of this job is sending young men off to ..." He let the words trail off. "Son, it's hardest when the men are as young as you. I know—we all know—that some men who go off to war don't come back. It's difficult for me to live with the fact that I'm making arrangements to send you into combat, knowing that that decision may very well cost you your life."

"I'll be fine, sir. And besides, it wasn't your decision. It was mine. I enlisted because I want to do my duty."

He stood up. "I'm sure even if your mother didn't approve of you enlisting, she's still proud of you."

I could only hope that would be the case.

"I want you to know that I'm proud of you." He stood up and offered a salute. "Dismissed ... Leading Aircraftman McWilliams."

I stood up and returned his salute. He then reached out and shook my hand.

10

I looked anxiously up and down the platform. Where was Chip? The train was going to leave in a few minutes, and if he didn't show up soon, I'd miss him completely. I stood up on the step of the car so I could get a better view of the whole platform. It was filled with soldiers, sailors, and flyers, either standing together in groups or separately with their families or wives. It looked as if the whole armed forces were on the move and passing through Union Station today.

The only people I'd had to say goodbye to were my new buddies at Manning, especially Jim and Johnnie. True, we hadn't known each other that long, but all things considered, it almost felt as though we'd been through a war together already. Goodbye was a firm handshake, a pat on the back, congratulations on my success, a few jokes about meeting up again on the "other side of the pond." No one wanted to make a big deal out of goodbyes in the military—there were too many of them.

It was impossible to travel—impossible to go anywhere—without bumping into somebody in uniform. We weren't a big country—Canada's population wasn't quite 12 million, compared with more like 136 million in the United States—but I'd heard that almost a million of us were in the armed forces, fighting against the Nazis.

In the crowded station, with everybody coming and going, maybe Chip couldn't find the right platform or find me. There were so many men in uniform and we all looked the—

"Chip!" I screamed.

He looked up, scanning the crowd. I waved to him. He saw me and waved back. I jumped down and ran toward him, dodging people on the platform. I threw my arms around him and gave him a big hug.

"My goodness, my man, let me have a look at you!" he exclaimed, and stepped back. "You've gained weight."

"Ten pounds."

"And have you grown? You look taller."

"It's more the thick boots," I said, lifting one of my feet for him to see. "I think it's more likely I've been worn down!"

"So how does it feel, you know, going overseas?" he asked.

"Great ... good." Chip was the one person who knew the

truth, so it didn't seem right to lie to him. "Actually I'm a little scared."

"If it was me, I'd be a *lot* scared. Me and you sitting around our dorm at school talking about going over to fight is a whole different thing from actually shipping over."

"I know. It's really happening."

"Honest, Robbie—I mean Davie, sorry—part of me is jealous beyond words. You get to join the fighting, while the only battles I'm waging are with my history teacher."

"From your letters, at least it sounds like you're getting along better with Beamish these days."

"I *was* getting along with him."

"Was? What happened?"

"For starters, I'm skipping class today to meet you."

"I'm so sorry! I didn't think of that!" I exclaimed.

"Not to worry. I had to do something. He was threatening to pull me out of the mailroom early because I'd been doing so 'bloody well' in my studies. Can't have that, old man. Going AWOL should keep me in the doghouse—and in the mailroom—for the rest of the year."

"Thanks so much, Chip. I really appreciate the sacrifice you're making."

"You appreciate *my* sacrifice? You're the one going off to

war! So, tell me, is it true—do the ladies love a man in uniform?"

"You know me. I'm not the type to kiss and tell."

"You're not even the type to *kiss*! But don't worry, some nice woman will eventually take pity and go out on a date with you."

"Thanks for the vote of confidence."

"No problem. That's what friends are for. So, you said they're making you a navigator."

"Yeah. I've been assigned to a Lancaster group."

"Lancs! How exciting. That's one beautiful bird! You'll be raining down death on Hitler's factories and forces!"

"Assuming I can find my way to the bomb sites. But I'll try to be the best navigator I can be … for now. I'll be able to apply for transfer to flight school after one tour."

"How long will that take?"

"Between six and twelve months."

"So, technically, I could enlist and become a pilot as quickly as you," Chip said. "Who knows, you might even be *my* navigator."

"Sorry, I'm afraid I'm not acting as the navigator on any plane where you're the pilot."

"Well, maybe I don't want to fly any plane where *you're* the navigator. You might land us in Berlin, for all I know."

"I might, assuming you didn't crash before we got there."

He gave me a playful punch on the shoulder. "You know I'd be proud to have you either as my navigator or flying the plane beside me in formation."

"I know. And there's nobody I'd rather fly with."

This was all getting far too maudlin and emotional. I pulled out the letters I'd written on the train. "Here are the next three letters for my mother."

"Why so many?"

"I'm going into a theatre of combat. All my letters back are now subject to being opened, read, and censored, so I can't risk pretending I'm still in school."

"I hadn't even thought of that," Chip admitted.

"I'll still write to you and tell you what I'm doing and where I'm going, but I've got to figure out a way to get letters through to you for you to send to my mother."

"Maybe you could hide a letter inside a parcel."

"No good. That would only make a censor more suspicious. Parcels are sent overseas to military men—not back home from men in uniform."

"I hadn't thought of that. There must be some way to get a letter through."

"I'll try to think of something. In the meantime, I'll still write letters to my mother for you to pass along, but they'll say very little, nothing that would suggest either that I'm in the air force or that I'm in boarding school. Just make sure she gets these letters when she's supposed to receive them."

I took one of the letters back and opened the flap. In light pencil strokes I'd written the date it should be mailed. "This one is particularly important. This explains why I won't be home for Christmas."

"I was wondering how you were going to explain that one."

"I'm hospitalized. Nothing too serious, a bit of pneumonia, not life-threatening, but I'm in quarantine. Always at least a slight risk that it could be TB, so there's no point in her coming to see me. You are going home for Christmas, aren't you? You could deliver it by hand?"

"Of course, although now you're making me feel guilty."

"Don't. None of this would be possible without you. When you deliver the letter, could you please give my mother and sisters a big hug for me, shake my brother's hand and tell him to listen to our mother, and ... tell them all that I love them?"

"You can count on me."

"I *have* been counting on you."

"How long before you're in England?"

"I arrive in Halifax tomorrow evening and then head straight down to the *Queen Mary*. She sails the next day, and it's a four- or five-day passage, depending on the seas and the route she takes."

"I've heard that Hitler has a bounty out on that ship."

"I heard that too. A quarter of a million dollars and the awarding of the Iron Cross to the U-boat captain who sinks her. But that's why she's so fast and well protected. We'll be fine."

"Yeah. The only danger you'll face is from seasickness."

"I'm sure you're right. As soon as I've settled in, I'll write you a note, tell you my mailing address—although I might not be able to tell you exactly where I'm stationed because of censorship issues."

"I understand. I'll wait for your letter and take care of these"—he held up the envelopes—"until then."

"All aboard!" the porter yelled out.

I felt a surge of electricity shoot up my spine. This was it.

"You keep yourself safe," Chip said as he offered his hand and we shook.

"I'll try."

"Don't just try—succeed. By the time I get over there, I want to make sure I've got an old hand who can lead me around and show me the ropes."

"I'll do my best."

He let go of my hand and saluted. I awkwardly saluted back.

"I'd best be going," he said.

"Yes, don't want to keep old Beamish waiting."

I could see there were tears in his eyes. I wasn't far from tears myself.

"Godspeed, old chap," Chip said. He turned and walked away.

"Thank you," I said under my breath. "Thank you for everything."

I grabbed my bag and hopped up onto the first step. From that vantage point I could see all along the platform. There were so many men saying their final goodbyes and getting ready to board the train. Others were already aboard and were leaning out of windows; arms reaching down met arms reaching up so that a final bit of contact could take place. I couldn't help but wonder how many of these goodbyes would be for the whole war. Or forever.

11

"We've sighted land!"

I looked up from my reading. It was one of my bunkmates, Campbell. Twelve of us—ten soldiers plus me and Campbell, the only two in the air force—shared a small stateroom, with four triple bunk beds. I put down my manual—it was an advanced text on navigation—and jumped off my bed. It was a long way from the very top. It seemed to be my destiny always to be on the top bunk. I was just hoping the bunks wouldn't be four high the next time!

Two of the other guys had gotten off their bunks as well, and the four of us went out into the corridor. There was no door to close behind us because all of the stateroom doors had been removed to make more space. The only doors that remained on the whole ship were either waterproof doors or those for the few staterooms that carried high-ranking officers or dignitaries. I'd been told that Winston Churchill, England's prime minister, had travelled on this ship. I figured *he* hadn't slept on the top bunk of a triple bed.

We entered the stairwell. It was bare concrete. All of the carpeting had been stripped away—too much of a hazard if the ship caught fire. We climbed the stairs, level by level. We were eleven floors below deck. Low-ranking servicemen got the lower floors. I guess I shouldn't have complained—at least we had a room. Other men were sleeping in bunks that had been placed on the Promenade Deck or, even worse, in the swimming pool! It had been drained, of course, the way the whole ship had been drained of all its finery. I could only imagine what it would have been like with all the expensive china, crystal, tablecloths, and fancy chandeliers it had before the war.

At each turn we passed another group of men either playing cards or shooting craps. Gambling wasn't allowed—officially—but there were pots of money visible at all of the games. Of course, I hadn't been involved with anything like that. I'd tried to keep to myself as much as possible. Besides, the CO at flight school had given me advanced navigation textbooks and flight manuals for the Lancaster before I left, and I swore I'd have them practically memorized before I reached the base. I was going to be the youngest, the least trained, and the most inexperienced person there, and I knew I'd have to work harder than everybody else if I wanted to show I belonged … which, of course, I really didn't.

We made our way out onto the deck. The air was cool—
no, it was *cold*—but it still felt very good in my lungs and
on my face. I could taste the salt in the air, but at least the
ride was a lot smoother now. For the first two days, we'd
experienced rough seas and a lot of men had been under the
weather. That wasn't so bad for those of us in the army or
the air force, but it was a bit embarrassing for a sailor to be
hanging over the railing throwing up into the ocean.

The whole starboard railing was lined with men.
Obviously that was the side for viewing. We walked along,
looking for an opening.

The deck, which once would have held deck chairs, was
lined with lifeboats—enough to accommodate the 16,000
passengers who now filled the ship beyond any capacity the
designers had ever dreamed of or planned for. I'd gotten
to know those boats well. Every single day of our passage
had been marked by two exercises: a lifeboat drill and an
abandon-ship drill. I knew these activities weren't just a way
to pass the time but something that could save our lives. Just
like with all the drills they made us do in basic training, they
wanted us to be able to act quickly, without thinking, if the
need arose.

Above us, on the upper deck, were the armaments that
had been added to the ship. There were six three-inch,

low-angle guns, two dozen single-barrel 20-millimetre cannons, and four sets of two-inch rocket launchers on the stern. It was an impressive array of weaponry. Of course, it was all designed to defend against an attack from the air or from surface vessels, and neither of those was what we needed to fear. The only real dangers were those that were unseen—the U-boats that could be anywhere beneath the waves. The best defence the *Queen Mary* had against U-boats—other than the escort vessels—was her speed and camouflage. The *Queen* had been painted navy grey, and her nickname was the Grey Ghost because of the way she'd been impossible for the U-boats to find as she sped across the ocean, changing course continually, zigzagging so no U-boat could get in front of her.

We found an opening at the railing, and the four of us squeezed in. On the horizon was the coast. It was far enough away that we couldn't make out much detail other than some colours—greens and greys and browns—but close enough to be reassuring. It looked as though we were paralleling the shore, but it was impossible to judge distance. We could be five miles out or we could be thirty.

"Looks like the *Queen Mary* got through again," Campbell said.

"Don't count your chickens until they're hatched," a sailor just over from him said. "We've still got a lot of ocean before we reach port."

Instinctively I looked down at the water and scanned it for periscopes. That had been my habit during the entire trip whenever I was on deck and at the railing. All I'd ever seen were rolling seas and the outlines of our escorts and other ships in the convoy. It was reassuring to see them now, even closer than usual.

"I wouldn't imagine any U-boat captain would be crazy enough to come this close to the mainland," Campbell said. "It's not just the escort vessels in our convoy but all the reconnaissance flights going over. He'd be seen the first time he poked up a periscope."

"Do you have any idea how hard it is to see a periscope?" one of the sailors asked. "It's one bloody big sea and one tiny little tube sticking out."

"What would it matter?" Campbell replied. "The *Queen Mary* makes thirty knots at full steam. Are you telling me there's a U-boat that can hope to match that? She'd just outrun it."

"Do you think the U-boat is going to ram our ship?" the sailor asked, barely hiding the contempt in his voice. "And do you really think the *Queen Mary* can outrun a torpedo?"

He and his friends began laughing. "Good thing we don't take advice from the *air force* about subs," he said with disdain.

I had a pretty good idea where this was going to end. There had been lots of little skirmishes during the passage. You put this many men in too small a space and don't give them anything to do, and you've got the basic ingredients for trouble. Then add in alcohol, gambling for high stakes, and members of the army, navy, and air force all mixed in together, and you're almost guaranteed trouble.

I did a quick head count of the crowd. Most of the men around us were army. They were the guys in khaki uniforms, and they were by far the majority on the ship. The rest of the men were mostly sailors—in the navy blue uniforms. This sailor had two buddies and there were a couple more navy blues down the way. The sailors were probably the worst for fighting. I looked around for the lighter-blue air force uniform, but aside from me and Campbell, there weren't any fly boys to be seen. Maybe Campbell would just let that comment go past without—

"Good thing the air force is there to watch over you from above," Campbell retorted. "Without us, you and your little bathtub toys would go down the drain."

Great, just what we needed—a skirmish this close to the

end of the voyage. The sailor came forward and I stepped between them.

"Look, boys," I said, "how about if we agree that the navy and the air force work together to keep the convoy safe. It's a partnership, right?"

The sailor looked down at me and scowled. This was not going to end well. Maybe I should get in the first punch before he got in the last. No, maybe not just yet. I decided to give it another try.

"I just don't want any Nazi looking through his periscope and seeing us fighting amongst ourselves. How about if you sailors join us members of the air force for a drink to celebrate reaching England?"

His scowl dissolved into a look of thoughtfulness.

"I'm buying," I said.

He broke into a big smile. "Why didn't you say so!" He slapped me on the back. "We'd be honoured to share a drink with the fine gentlemen of the air force."

He offered Campbell his hand and they shook.

"As long as we don't have to spend any more time with army grunts," the sailor said.

A couple of the soldiers standing nearby heard his words and reacted.

"Yeah, no army, just members of the two *elite* branches of

the military," Campbell said. "If we want the army to come, we'll just whistle like we're calling a—"

"I think there's room at the table for everybody," I interjected. I pulled out some money. "Would you gentlemen like to join us?" I said to the soldiers. "My treat, so we can hoist a glass to toast the successful crossing of the Grey Ghost."

"Thanks," one of the soldiers said. He turned to his friends. "Come on, boys, the drinks are on the fly boy!"

Seven or eight soldiers broke into smiles and cheered. I wanted to say that I'd only invited a couple of them, but that would have started a fight for sure. Besides, lots of men had spent most of their pay on alcohol; I'd just be the first to do it without drinking anything himself.

"Let's go, boys," I said. "He's right, the drinks are on the fly boy."

12

"Leading Aircraftman McWilliams reporting for duty, sir!" I said, snapping to attention.

"Have a seat," the CO said without looking up from the clutter on his desk. He had a thick English accent, a thicker moustache, and eyebrows that matched. He looked as though he was old enough to have kids older than me.

I looked around. The only seats were already occupied with piles of paper. Carefully I scooped up some of the papers and placed them on the floor and sat down.

My new commanding officer—Group Captain Matthews—continued to work. I looked around. The walls of the room were filled with maps of Europe, charts, and the names of pilots and their crews. I started to count. There had to be seventy or eighty bomber crews stationed at this base.

Group Captain Matthews looked up at me from the work on his desk and his eyes widened in surprise. I knew what he was going to say next.

"How old are you, son?" he asked, sounding incredulous.

"Old enough to fight, sir."

He chuckled. "That wasn't the question, son. How old *are* you?"

"Eighteen on my last birthday, sir."

"Well, that would make you nineteen on your next birthday, which would still make you the youngest person on this base." He shook his head. "We're desperate for navigators, but I was hoping for somebody who had more experience than simply being able to find his way home from school."

"I understand your concern, sir, but I won't let you down."

"It's not me I'm worried about. You have never been on a combat mission."

"No, sir."

"You can tone down that 'sir' stuff as well. Please, not so often, or at least not so loud. We're a little less formal here at the front."

"Yes, sir ... I mean, yes."

He let out a big sigh. "Okay, let me look at your transfer papers."

He started shuffling papers around on his desk, moving piles from one side to the other, but it didn't look as though he was having any luck. I glanced down at the floor to the papers I'd just moved. On the top of one pile was a manila folder, and in large letters the label read *McWilliams, David*.

I picked it up. "Is this what you're looking for, sir?"

He took it. "Yes, it is, but why did you have it?"

"I didn't. It was here … on the floor."

"Oh, good. At least it was somewhere in my office." He opened the file up. "Oh, goodness, it says here that you've not yet even completed your training as a navigator."

"No, sir. They said I'd receive my final training here, sort of on-the-job."

"Wonderful. So instead of sending me a navigator, they sent me somebody who might someday grow up to be a navigator."

"Sir, I will work hard to become the best navigator you have."

He chuckled. "I like that confidence, but may I suggest that you don't make that claim in the presence of the other navigators?"

"I'll try to remember that."

"Well, for better or worse, you're what we've got. Ask my clerk to bring you to the supply room to be issued your flight suit, chow down in the mess hall, and then report to the briefing room at nineteen hundred hours. I'll assign you to a navigator who will supervise and coordinate your ongoing training."

"Thank you, sir," I said, jumping to my feet and saluting.

He gave me a little wave that was sort of like a salute. "And don't be late. We'll be in the air by twenty hundred and over France within three hours of that."

"I'm going out with the crew tonight?"

"I don't know any other way to train and test you." He paused and looked at me as though he was deep in thought. "You seem a little surprised."

"I guess a bit ... I just didn't think I'd be going out so soon."

"The faster we train you, the sooner you can be on your own. The war isn't waiting for you to be trained. Now get moving, you only have forty minutes."

The briefing room was filled with pilots, flight engineers, bomb aimers, and navigators. There was a lot of loud conversation and laughter going on as the men milled around the room. I sat in the back, quiet, trying not to be noticed. Captain Matthews was at the front with his senior officers. He'd be leading the briefing.

I adjusted my new jacket—my flight jacket. It was leather

and had a thick lining. I felt very hot and wanted to slip it off, but all the other men were wearing theirs and I didn't want to stand out. Besides, I felt pretty proud to be wearing it ... proud, but maybe not worthy ... at least not yet.

All my clothes, right down to my felt flight boots, were designed to guard against the cold. We'd be flying at around fourteen thousand feet and the Lancasters weren't heated. A couple of guys had mentioned to me that it was so cold up at that altitude that I'd be able to see my breath. They joked that if you "bought it" up there, at least you could "see" your last breath.

"Okay, men, let's settle down!" Group Captain Matthews yelled out.

Instantly the room went completely silent. The men took their seats and opened up their flight journals. Everything was now business.

"Gentlemen, I would like to begin with a review of yesterday's raids. As you are aware, we joined with other squadrons in a mass assault involving 208 planes. The pathfinders did a first-rate job in marking our targets, and the aerial photographs taken by the recon units indicate that our barrage registered significant success."

"Does that mean we don't have to go back at those yards tonight, Skip?" one of the pilots asked.

"Looking for a new challenge, are we?" Matthews replied.

"I'm just starting to feel like I've been there so often, the enemy should invite me down for a spot of tea."

"And with the amount of archie they were throwing up at us, you could have practically walked down to the ground to get that tea," another pilot said, and there was a lot of laughter.

"The anti-aircraft fire was, as always, heavy," Group Captain Matthews agreed. "Of the eleven planes lost, seven of those were due to ack-ack. The remaining four planes were taken down by enemy fighters."

I'd already heard that three of those planes were from our squadron.

"Any word on our men?" an officer asked.

"Parachutes were seen exiting from *two* planes."

What he was saying was that the men in the other plane didn't get out, so they were dead.

"We have not received word indicating anything further on the men who parachuted from their planes. However, these days many more of our downed airmen are being assisted by locals and by members of the Resistance and have managed to avoid capture. At this point, we simply assume that no news is good news."

It had been three weeks from the day my father had been

shot down till the day we received word that he had been taken prisoner. We would never have conceived that my father being taken prisoner could be "good news," but it was. It meant that he was alive, and that's all that mattered.

I'd often thought about what it must have been like for him—being shot down, captured, and brought to a POW camp, where he'd been living now for the past two years. None of it seemed possible or real. I guess I wanted it to stay that way.

"Which reminds me, please make sure that you have your escape kit with you at all times!"

I had been issued mine. It was a small package that contained a silk map of France, a rubber water bottle, a few French phrases—Lord knows I wished I'd paid more attention in French class—a file, a compass, and some foreign currency, mostly French francs and German marks.

"I know that some of you are superstitious and feel that if you keep the escape kit on your person, you are somehow jinxing your plane. We are flying in Lancs, not on broomsticks, so there is no place for magical thinking. Keep the kits with you."

There was a little bit of grumbling around the room.

"That was not a suggestion," Group Captain Matthews boomed.

I was struck with a strange thought—of getting shot down and ending up in the same camp as my father, of he and I becoming bunkmates. That wasn't the family reunion either of us would have expected or wanted.

"We will be in the air by twenty hundred hours."

Matthews was leading the raid. He was no "penguin," which was the term given to squadron leaders who didn't fly in missions even though they had wings.

"There will be full fighter escort for the initial two hundred miles and they will be waiting for us upon our return. It will be a full circus tonight."

I leaned over to the officer beside me. "What's a circus?" I whispered.

"A circus is when we have a mix of bombers and fighters. A rodeo is when the groups operate alone."

"Thanks."

Matthews continued. "We will be taking a vectored course with two mid-flight course corrections. Your navigators have already been given that information to make plot changes. Please make these changes in unison. Our best defence against enemy planes is to stay together. We may not be in a tight formation, but being in the same area is essential."

He used a pointer to show the flight plan and the two course changes leading right to the target.

"Expect heavy anti-aircraft fire, as always. Once you've dropped your cookies, scramble out but try to remain on course. Stray planes present the easiest targets for enemy fighters. Your return route is direct and, as I said, full fighter coverage will escort us home as soon as we're in range."

Fighter planes had limited fuel capacity, so they weren't able to stay with bomber missions that went deep into enemy territory.

"What's the weather looking like?" somebody asked.

"Slight headwinds, which certainly will, of course, become tailwinds to aid in our escape, unlimited visibility, high ceiling, and, as we all know, almost a full moon tonight. There will be no place to hide but, by the same token, no place for enemy fighters to hide either. We should be able to see them coming, so gunners, eyes fully open for the entire mission, because we are counting on you.

"I'm going to be leading tonight's mission. Accompanying me will be the newest member of our squadron." He gestured in my direction. "McWilliams, stand up."

I slowly, awkwardly, got to my feet. Every eye was on me. I felt so self-conscious. I figured I knew what they were all thinking.

"He'll be riding a few flights to get up to speed as a navigator before he's assigned to a crew. Do whatever you can to show him the ropes and make him feel like a member of our squadron."

"Good to have you aboard," one of the airmen said.

"Welcome!" said another, and there was a round of applause.

I nodded my head, gave a little wave, and settled back into my seat.

"Dismissed, men."

13

I stood in the cockpit behind Group Captain Matthews and the flight engineer as they were going over their pre-flight checklist. Matthews was behind the yoke and the flight engineer was to his right, where he could monitor the gauges.

"We'll start with the inner starboard tank," the flight engineer said.

Despite having been introduced to him just ten minutes earlier on the tarmac, I couldn't remember his name.

"Check," Matthews said. "And then switch to the inside port fuel tank."

"Will do, Cap."

I looked down past the flight engineer's feet and could make out the outline of our bomb aimer. His perch was underneath the controls in the very nose of the plane in a little glass bubble. I wasn't afraid of heights—I *liked* heights—but still, staring down through nothing but glass held in place with a few strips of metal seemed a little much even for me.

Directly behind me, the navigator—Mike—sat at a little table, his maps and charts spread out in front of him. Behind him, past a little curtain, I could see both the wireless operator and the legs of the top gunner, hanging down from his turret. Lost from view at the very back of the plane was the tail gunner. His turret was a bubble like the bomb aimer's.

I turned and looked down the tarmac. If I'd wanted to, I could have counted two or three dozen planes, all waiting, preparing, getting ready to go into battle. There was something so incredible about being here in the middle of it all. *I was here.* I was going to take part in what I'd read about, heard about, watched on the newsreels. Maybe I wasn't going to be the pilot—heck, I wasn't even going to be the navigator—but I was finally going to strike a blow against the Nazis. It felt good, and unreal, and amazing, and unnerving.

I was feeling hot. Between my sweater, leather jacket, life jacket, and harness, I was sweating. I knew it was supposed to get cold up there, but I couldn't imagine I'd need to wear the wool hat and gloves I'd been issued. Actually, for the navigator, wouldn't gloves make it difficult to do the calculations?

Anxiously, absently, I played with the straps of my harness. My parachute—which would be hooked to the harness if needed—was just off to the side in a neat pile with those of the pilot, flight engineer, and navigator. The other crew members' parachutes were closer to where they were stationed—and by their escape hatches. In an emergency, they wouldn't be able to travel the length of the plane to retrieve anything. A few seconds could mean the difference between life and death ...

Death. I let that sink in a little.

Tonight, on this mission, people could die. People *would* die. That was all but guaranteed. I knew in some theoretical, abstract way that it could even be me, but the lack of reality almost protected me from thinking any deeper.

"Is this your first bombing mission?" Mike asked. He had a thick accent—not British, maybe Australian or South African.

"This is my first time in a Lancaster."

"Really? What were you flying in before?"

"A couple of different things." I didn't want him to know that those things were small planes piloted by my father.

"The Lanc is a good plane," he said. "Very stable platform. She flies so gently, it'll practically rock you to sleep."

"I don't think I'm going to be doing any sleeping."

"Good. Maybe that means I can catch a few extra winks along the way."

"You don't actually fall asleep, do you?"

He laughed. "Not likely. But I do close my eyes and think about being somewhere else ... usually someplace that's warm and sunny."

"Contact!" Matthews said.

One of the engines—the outside starboard—flickered, sputtered, and then puffed out a cloud of smoke and came to life with a tremendous roar.

"Contact!" he yelled again.

The outside port engine responded and the noise increased.

Matthews and the flight engineer repeated their words and actions until all four engines were firing. The noise was unbelievable and the whole plane shook.

"Purrs like a kitten, don't she?" Mike yelled over the din of the engines.

"Sounds more like the roar of a lion!"

"Nah, it should sound more like music to your ears. It's when you *don't* hear the engines that you need to get worried!"

The plane jerked slightly, rocked, and then started to roll forward. I looked out through the canopy, past the pilot and flight engineer. In front of us were two other planes already moving down the tarmac, taxiing into position for takeoff. I turned around. Behind us, the other planes were falling into line. This was all becoming more real by the second.

Mike had put on headphones and handed me a pair. I slipped them on and the noise was partially blocked out and—

"We can talk on the intercom," Mike said.

"Good ... good." I was relieved that I could hear him so well despite the overwhelming noise of the engine.

"Just not too much chatter," Captain Matthews said, cutting in. "And definitely no singing."

Almost instantly, a voice started singing and two others joined in until there was a choir chirping out a song that I didn't know. I wondered how the captain would feel about the men disobeying his order not to sing. I looked up. He was one of the choir members. They finished the song and there was silence.

"There's the signal," Matthews said.

Mike leaned in closer to me. "The Aldis lamps on the runway turn green when we're good to go."

"Okay, boys, hold on to your hats!"

I stood up and leaned against the flight engineer's chair so that I could see everything inside and outside the plane.

With his right hand Matthews pushed all four of the throttle controls forward and the noise of the engines became even louder. The plane started to pick up speed. The tarmac wasn't nearly as smooth as I'd thought it would be, and the whole plane was shaking and vibrating. The ride got even bumpier as our speed increased. It felt like either the fillings in my teeth would fall out or the wings would fall off. Faster and faster, but we weren't getting off the ground. The end of the runway was up ahead and beyond that some trees and a church ... Why was there a church steeple at the end of a runway?

I felt a rush of anxiety. Were we going to make it? Was the plane going to lift off or were we going to crash into the forest or—

All at once the ride became incredibly smooth and we were gaining elevation! We soared up and the trees passed below, and then the church steeple vanished beneath us. We were quickly gaining altitude—much faster than I'd expected.

I stumbled, almost tumbling over, grabbing on to the back of the flight engineer's seat to stop myself, as the plane banked sharply to the right. Below us I could see the barracks and the runway and other planes taxiing out to join us. Matthews levelled the plane out, taking us on a long circular path around the field. We joined into a formation with those already in the air, marshalling for those still to come.

"This is beautiful," I said quietly.

"That it is," Matthews replied.

"Sorry, sir, I was just talking to myself."

"You'll have to learn to do that in your head." He paused. "How are the gauges looking?"

"Engine temperatures are within the normal range. All systems are go," the flight engineer replied.

"Excellent. That's what I like to hear, old chap. Okay, crew, we're going to give it a go tonight. I want everybody to stay sharp, stay focused on the task. Understood?"

There were grunts of agreement coming back through the headphones from different places in the plane. I'd stay sharp too, although I wasn't sure if I was anything more than luggage at this stage.

I looked out the canopy window. We were in a sea of Lancasters, with planes surrounding us on all sides. I knew there were two hundred planes on this mission, but it seemed as if there were thousands. They filled the sky in all directions, illuminated by the stars and the bright moonlight, until the edges of the formation were swallowed up in the darkness.

Along with the bombers were the escort fighter planes. Most were Spitfires—the type of plane my father had flown. The type of plane I hoped to fly someday. As they darted past, they seemed so fast and nimble and small compared with the big, lumbering Lancasters. It was good to have them along, but they only made me realize how vulnerable we would be to enemy fighter attacks. They just zipped between us, so much faster, and they were able to manoeuvre, turn, climb, and bank much more quickly than we possibly could. I wondered how much longer they'd be with us before they had to turn back.

I knew, from the conversations I heard on the intercom system, that we had passed over the English Channel and that below us was occupied France. So far we hadn't encountered any enemy aircraft or anti-aircraft fire—not that either was expected at this point. Anti-aircraft fire would be placed around target areas to offer protection from the bombing, and enemy fighters wouldn't attack until our escorts had turned back.

"Course correction coming up, right?" I asked the navigator.

"Soon. You have a knack for this. Any visuals below that you can make out?"

I shook my head. The last thing I'd seen with any clarity was the white cliffs of Dover, and since then there'd been nothing.

"It's hard at night, especially when everything is blacked out. When the runs are during the day, you'll see more. No matter how much you trust your maps, your memory, and your mathematics, it's always good to take a reckoning off landmarks."

"He's telling you the truth there."

I thought it was the flight engineer talking.

"Same as my job. Read your dials, but use your head."

It *was* the flight engineer. I had to remember to find out his name.

"I've seen engineers so focused on their dials that they didn't notice an engine was on fire because the heat indicator said everything was fine."

"I'll try to remember that … There's so much to remember," I replied.

"He's doing a tremendous job!" Mike said. "I think I'll leave him to do the job himself. Anybody mind if I step out for a smoke?"

There was laughter over the intercom.

"Come on, Mikey, you know there's no smoking close to the aircraft. Don't want to go setting off the oxygen tanks," somebody said over the intercom.

"I suppose that's the end of my other idea—to light a bonfire to warm my hands," Mike said.

There was more laughter, but I would have welcomed the bonfire. It was so cold now that I was able to see my breath, and I'd put on both my wool cap and my gloves.

"Okay, everybody, not only shouldn't we be lighting fires, but it's time to extinguish all lights," Captain Matthews said over the PA. "We're about to lose our fighter coverage."

Mike dimmed the light over his table and we were plunged into darkness. The only faint light came from the dials on the instrument panel. Slowly my eyes adjusted and I was able to see outlines.

"Are the bombs selected and fused?" Matthews asked.

"Yes, sir, Cap. Bombs selected and fused. If you like, we can drop them right here and return to base immediately."

There was more laughter.

"I'm afraid that would set a record for creepback," Matthews said.

I'd heard about creepback—a plane dropping its bombs well short of the target to escape the flak.

"I think we'll stick with the original plan and drop them on target instead of over the French countryside."

"Affirmative on that, Captain. Just like to give you options."

"I wish I had the option of longer fighter coverage," the captain said, "but there they go."

I stood up so I could look out the canopy. Off to the starboard side and up about forty-five degrees, I could make out the outlines of two Spitfires. The first one climbed high above us while the second waggled its wings—waving goodbye—and then dove sharply and disappeared.

I looked all around. There were no more Spitfires to be seen. I could still see the outlines of lots of Lancasters, though. Those close and to the port side, the side with the moon, were almost shining and shimmering in the moonlight, while others, farther away, were just dark shapes in the night sky. It was reassuring to know we weren't alone, and we certainly weren't defenceless, but this was where the dangerous part of the mission began. This was when the enemy fighters would be coming up after us.

"Time for course correction," Mike said. "I want you to change bearings ... fifteen degrees north."

"Roger that," Matthews said. "I'm also changing

altitude ... climbing to eighteen-five ... I see some cloud cover we can climb into."

I felt the plane slowly bank at the same time as it began its climb. It was a gentle, smooth course change. I could only barely feel it, and a hand against the navigator's table held me in place

"Feeling okay, kid?" Mike asked.

"I guess so. Anything I can do to help?"

"Go to the back for a while. Make sure the tail gunner is staying sharp ... Even keep an eye out. Watch below and behind, because that's the most likely direction of attack."

"Sure. No problem."

I started to walk toward the back, but he grabbed me by the arm and stopped me. He pointed to the floor, and for a second I didn't realize what he meant. Then it clicked in. I reached down and picked up my parachute.

14

"Navigator, how long until we're over the target?" Group Captain Matthews asked.

Mike motioned for me to answer.

"Six minutes, sir," I replied.

"Has Mike gone out for that smoke?" Matthews asked.

"Still here, Skip. Just letting the kid earn his wings."

"Any lights up front?" Matthews asked.

There were pathfinder planes that would hit the target before us, flying low and dropping flares first to mark the target and then firebombs to light it up.

"Negative, Skip." It was the bomb aimer.

Hanging there in the bubble at the front of the plane, he had the best view. I started to wonder, had I given us the wrong heading? I knew that one degree off projected over a couple of hundred miles would cause us to miss the target by ten miles, and we'd made five different course changes under my direction.

"Mike?" the captain asked.

"We're right on course. The kid is bang on. I've already had him plot our return path."

"And you've confirmed everything?" Matthews asked.

He sounded concerned. I didn't blame him, because he wasn't the only one who wondered about my abilities. I wasn't willing to trust the safety of the crew to me without my calculations being double-checked. Chip joking about me landing us in Berlin still stuck in my head.

"Confirmed, plotted, and marked. The kid is a natural."

"The jury is still out on whether he can be a navigator or not, but I'm thinking of making him into my personal good luck charm. We're almost over the target and no sightings of enemy fighters the whole trip. How often does that happen?"

"Not very often—certainly not often enough," Mike replied.

"This is starting to look like a milk run!"

"We have archie! I repeat, we have archie to the port side!" the bomb aimer yelled out over the intercom. "It's set for about twelve or thirteen thousand!"

"I see it," Matthews announced. "I'm going to put a little distance between it and us."

I felt the plane climb and bank simultaneously. At the same time there was a loud explosion and the whole aircraft shook. There was another explosion and another, and the plane shuddered.

Mike leaned over so his mouth was right by my ear. "This isn't so bad. Once the flak starts, it's a guarantee that no fighters are in the area!" he yelled over the sound of the engines. "Let's just drop our cookies and get out of here."

"I see the markers!" the bomb aimer yelled out.

It was essential to have the target marked, but it also marked *us*—where exactly we were heading. Everybody on the ground, all the anti-aircraft gunners, and the planes they could send up to intercept us—all knew we were coming. I guess that didn't really make much difference, though. Between radar and a cloudless, moonlit night, they probably knew anyway.

"Forward ... one minute ... level it out."

The plane came out of the bank and flattened out.

"Opening bomb doors," the flight engineer announced.

I heard the hydraulics and felt the plane slow down slightly as the open bomb doors caused more drag. I knew that once the bombs were dropped we'd be so much lighter that we'd be able to fly faster and climb more quickly—and we'd need that if the fighters did come up after us.

I stood up so I could look out through the canopy. All around us the sky was starting to fill with black puffs, exploding anti-aircraft fire, and powerful searchlights were sweeping the sky looking for us. Up ahead, the flak looked thicker and closer together, and that's where we were flying—where they knew we were going to be flying. Despite the bitter cold, my whole body suddenly felt a rush of heat, and sweat started pouring down the inside of my shirt.

"Two degrees to port … a little more … steady. Flat and level … Release the bombs on your mark."

"Roger that," Matthews replied.

"Roger, Skip. Twenty seconds to release," the bomb aimer replied.

He started counting down. I counted down in my head along with him, wanting him to count faster so we could release them quicker. Up ahead was more and more flak— and we were flying straight for it!

"Bombs away!" the bomb aimer called out.

The flight engineer pushed a lever forward. "The cookies are away!"

At the same instant that I heard them being released, the plane jumped up. I'd known that would happen, but I was surprised by how violent the leap upward was.

"Bomb doors closed," the engineer said.

"Evasive action! Hard to port!" the bomb aimer yelled. "Hard, hard, hard!"

It was almost as if the plane heard him and responded immediately. I wasn't ready for the quick response and tumbled off my chair and rolled across the floor. The engines whined and screamed as we turned, and then the plane suddenly dipped and dove! I rolled *up* the wall of the fuselage, rising almost all the way to the ceiling! The plane flattened out and I fell back down, luckily landing on the pile of parachutes.

Mike reached over and grabbed me, pulling me toward him. "Grab on to the table!" he yelled. "Wedge yourself underneath so you won't go bouncing around!"

He held on to me until I could get my legs locked around one of the legs of the table.

"Climb, climb, climb!" the bomb aimer yelled. "Get elevation—flak directly ahead. Hard to port, hard to port!"

The plane banked and climbed at the same time—a surefire way for an inexperienced pilot to stall or sideslip or … But I didn't have an inexperienced pilot—the squadron leader was at the controls of this plane.

There was a thunderous explosion and the plane shook violently. Had we been hit? Should I grab my parachute? I looked over at Mike. He wasn't moving. He wasn't even reacting. He was completely calm. In fact, was there a little smile on his face? He had his head down and was studying the charts in front of him. That made no sense. How could he be so calm?

Mike looked up. He gave me a thumbs-up and broke into a big grin. He leaned forward. "Quite the ride ... It's almost over ... Just hang tight."

The plane levelled out once again. The engines were loud, but they weren't whining anymore—there was a purring to them—and there was no more flak. Were we out of it?

"Clear, open sky ahead," the bomb aimer announced.

"Confirmed," Matthews agreed. "Clear sailing. All eyes external. Report Lancaster positions and ready for possible attack. What does it look like out there?"

"Scattered, very scattered formation."

I didn't recognize the voice but knew it had to be the wireless operator.

"We have planes port and starboard ... scattered elevations and directions."

"Time to get this formation back into shape," Group Captain Matthews said. "Mike, give me a bearing and elevation."

Mike instantly barked out a different bearing than the one I'd calculated. Had I been wrong? No, it was because the evasive action had spun us off course and he'd had to recalculate—something he'd done in the middle of all that chaos, the dips and banks and climbs amidst the barrage of anti-aircraft fire. When I'd been panicked, he'd been working, doing his job. Could I have done that job with all of that happening? Did I have what it took to be the brains of the plane?

There was a gentle turn as we banked to starboard, back toward the route I'd originally plotted.

"This is group leader to squadron pilots and navigators," Captain Matthews called out. "Let's re-form and tighten up, on my initial bearing and elevation. Let's get ready and ready fast. The way that flak stopped so suddenly, I expect we're going to have visitors soon. All eyes open. Gunners be awake, be aware, be active."

Mike leaned forward again. "Every plane had to take individual evasive action to avoid the flak, so they're scattered across the sky. Until we get back into a tighter formation, we're more vulnerable to enemy fighters."

"So once we get into formation, we're safe?"

He chuckled. "Safer, not safe. Go back and ask Sparky if he knows how many planes were lost."

"Planes were lost?"

"Planes are always lost. What we don't know is how many. Go—he'll know."

Hesitantly I got up from the table, reluctant to leave,

fearing that a sudden change in direction would throw me across the plane. Then I remembered: Captain Matthews was going to be flying flat and straight to allow everybody else to re-form around him. At least that was the plan, unless we were attacked by enemy fighter planes. I'd better hurry.

I moved through the plane, one hand steadying myself against the wall. Sparky—which seemed to be what every wireless operator was called—was busy working, listening on his headphones and tapping out a message in Morse code to the other planes. He looked up at me.

"How many planes?" I yelled.

He shook his head. "None yet … No enemy fighters yet."

"No, no, how many of our planes were … were …" I let the sentence trail off, as if asking the question would somehow increase the number.

"Eight … seven … I don't know for sure. There are reports of at least five being downed, and others that haven't reported in or—" He stopped and his eyes got big and his expression even more serious. "We have confirmed enemy contact. A dozen echoes on the fishpond so far."

I knew that "fishpond" was the nickname for radar, and "echoes" meant there were planes on that radar.

"Where are they?" Matthews called out over the intercom.

"Climbing from the stern and port … four o'clock … five o'clock … gaining quickly."

"Does anybody see them?" Matthews inquired. "Anybody in any plane, do we have a visual?"

"Affirmative!" came a voice I didn't recognize. "We have visuals coming at us from below … dozens of them … dozens!" he screamed.

"Gunners be alive!"

At that same instant there was an explosion of gunfire! I spun around and saw the tail gunner swivelling in his turret, firing his gun! Then, from above, the upper gunner began firing, his legs spinning as he rotated his turret, spent cartridges being spat out and falling to the floor like rain, bouncing and rolling around. The air stunk of cordite, the smell of gunpowder.

I stood there paralyzed with fear. I didn't know what to do or where to go. I wanted to find someplace to hide, but there was no place to hide.

"Bandits, bandits, coming in from the front, diving on us, diving!" a voice cried out.

The feet of the upper gunner spun around as the turret swivelled and he readied himself. His movement unstuck me and I ran back to my spot by Mike. His head was down; he was working on a formula for a course correction.

He looked up. "Help provide another set of eyes."

I heard the words, but I didn't understand what he meant.

"Go forward!" he screamed, motioning to the front of the cockpit. "Look for enemy planes!"

"Oh, yeah."

I pushed past his table and brushed the curtain aside so I was standing right behind the pilot and flight engineer. Up above me—all around me—was the open glass of the canopy. If I was looking for someplace to hide, this wasn't it. Here, I was completely and utterly exposed.

I looked around. I could see the darkened images of Lancasters all around us. Dozens, no hundreds of planes flying in formation. But I couldn't see any—

A tiny plane zipped between two of the bombers just over to our port side, and red tracers streamed from its guns while the guns from three Lancasters spat fire back at it, bullets forming a path from their guns out into the air. The plane twisted and turned and sped by so fast, it was as if the bullets couldn't even catch it! It was untouched, but its bullets didn't seem to be hitting their targets either, as we kept on flying steady and level.

"There! There!" I screamed. Directly in front, flying straight toward us, was another fighter, and its guns were blazing! Red tracers came flying out from overhead—our upper gun was firing at it! Our plane dipped and the fighter flew overhead, so close that I could see the rivets in the bottom of his wing!

Involuntarily I leaned back and almost fell over.

"Close ... a bit closer than I would have liked," Matthews said. His voice was so calm, so matter-of-fact. "Good eyes, Davie! You really are a good luck charm."

I didn't feel so lucky. All I felt was my heart pounding, my legs shaking, sweat pouring down my sides, and I thought there was a chance I might throw up. I wanted to sit down, I wanted to curl up into a little ball, but I couldn't. I grabbed on to the canopy to steady myself and began scanning the sky again.

15

The wheels screeched as the plane touched down and then bounced slightly back into the air, causing my legs to jam into the bottom of the table. We raced along the tarmac, and the roar of the engines and the rattling of the runway diminished as we slowed down until we were merely rolling, taxiing toward the hangar.

The two gunners were out of their turrets now, and Sparky was off the wireless, and they were all standing together. I couldn't hear them over the engines, but they were laughing and smiling. It was so strange ... they were acting as if nothing had happened! Or maybe they were just so relieved that it was over. I was relieved too, but also numb. Mike was packing up the maps into a leather carrying case.

Finally the engines stopped, so suddenly that I was startled and then relieved. I unplugged my headphones and took them off. Now I could hear the voices and the laughter. The hatch popped open and they all climbed out, parachutes in hands. I stayed in my seat. I felt so drained that I wasn't sure my legs would hold me up.

"How you doing?" Mike asked.

"I'm okay. I'm okay."

"You did well. Didn't he do well, Skipper?"

Matthews held out a hand. "Congratulations on your first mission. You performed admirably."

"I didn't do much."

"You got us back home," Mike said. "Kid can plot my course any time."

"Thanks."

"Come on, everybody, let's get some breakfast before the debriefing," Group Captain Matthews said.

I slowly got to my feet. My legs felt like rubber and I hoped nobody noticed that I was wobbly and shaking—just as I hoped nobody had noticed the tears that I'd already shed. There hadn't been many, and I'd instantly brushed them away, but I couldn't stop them from coming. I'd been so relieved, so grateful, when the first Spitfires appeared and chased the last of the enemy planes away that the tears had just come.

For almost two hours we'd been repeatedly attacked by enemy fighter planes. They swooped by, attacking from above, below, behind, and straight ahead. Sometimes it had been only a few planes acting independently, and other times it had been a whole formation coming in. Our gunners had inflicted some damage. I hadn't seen it, but I'd heard over the radio that we had downed two, with a third being a probable kill.

But they weren't the only kills. I'd watched from the canopy as a Lancaster was strafed by enemy fire and then burst into flames, spun to the side, and plunged. It disappeared from my field of view before I could see if any of the crew had escaped. And that wasn't the only plane. I'd heard chatter over the radio and knew that at least another three planes had been shot out of the sky—another twenty-one men who wouldn't be coming back this morning.

There was a truck waiting by the plane. We climbed into the back, where our other three crew members were already waiting. Mike banged on the back of the cab to signal we were in, and the truck lurched forward, exhaust fumes spewing out and into the back. It brought back memories of that first truck ride on the way to the Manning Training School. Was that only two months ago? It seemed like years ago, when I was so much younger.

Everybody in the truck with me seemed so happy. The conversation was full of laughter and discussion around a football game scheduled for later that day between our squadron and another one and what they hoped to get for breakfast. My stomach was so upset I didn't know if I could eat, or keep it down if I did.

The truck came to a stop, but my stomach didn't. It seemed to be getting more and more upset and ... I was going to throw up!

"Let me through ... please," I pleaded as I pushed through and jumped off the truck, almost tumbling over as my feet hit the ground.

I ran on wobbly legs, almost falling over, until I reached the side of the building and then rushed to the back. I wanted to get out of sight before I vomited. The convulsions got so bad I doubled over and started heaving—loudly and violently. The chocolate and beef jerky I'd eaten during the flight came flooding back up, flowing out and down my face and onto my boots and the ground. I heaved again, and the little that remained came out. I struggled to get my breath, and my whole body was flushed, and I felt light-headed. I stumbled a couple of feet and dropped to my hands and knees. The grass was cool and wet with dew. I brought one hand up and held it against my forehead. The moisture felt good.

There was a hand on my back and I looked up. It was Group Captain Matthews.

"Feeling better?" he asked.

I wiped my mouth with the sleeve of my jacket. "A little bit … I'm … I'm sorry."

"Sorry about what?"

"About this … I just … my stomach … it was too much." I paused. "I don't know if I can do it."

"Do what? Have breakfast?"

"I don't know if I can do that either. But I meant fly … I was just so … so …"

"Scared?"

I looked down, away from him, and nodded my head in agreement.

"I'm scared every time I go up."

"You?" That caught me totally off guard. Then I realized why he'd said it. "I appreciate you trying to make me feel better, but I was up there. I saw. You weren't scared."

"When that plane came directly toward us, I almost screamed. If you're not scared when something like that happens, you have to be delusional, psychotic, or in extreme denial, and none of those apply to me."

"But you didn't look scared. You didn't act scared. Nobody did." I was thinking about Mike's calm demeanour and about the flight engineer monitoring the panel controls while bullets were flying all around us and enemy fighters were buzzing by.

"How we act and what we're feeling are different. You handled it well."

"This is handling it well?" I asked.

"Son, this was your first mission. I have men—grown men with wives and kids—who still bring up before or after or during each mission. Men, brave men whom I would trust with my life—men whom I *have* trusted with my life—who break down in tears, who wake up from a deep sleep in a cold sweat, screaming out in fear."

"Great. Is that what I have to look forward to?"

"Maybe you do."

That wasn't the reassuring answer I'd expected.

"I just don't know if I can handle it."

"I don't know either," he said. Again, a brutally honest answer, but not the one I'd been hoping for.

"What I do know is that you acquitted yourself well. I'm not one to blow smoke up your skirt. You followed orders, you reacted promptly, and, quite frankly, you saw that oncoming fighter before I did. If you hadn't ..." He shrugged. "Maybe there would have been one less plane heading home and somebody would be writing a letter to my wife."

He reached down and offered me a hand, helping me to my feet. "That's the hardest part of this job. It's my responsibility to write to inform the family about the fate of their loved one. Today is a good day—I only have fourteen letters to write."

"*Fourteen* ... that's how many died?" I knew that meant only two planes had gone down—at least, two from our squadron.

"I don't know yet for certain, but I believe there are eight confirmed deaths."

"How do you know that?"

"One plane went down without any sign of parachutes. From the other they saw six parachutes deploy, but the seventh was a Roman candle."

"I don't know what that means."

"His chute was on fire, burning as he was plummeting to the ground. Poor bugger—better to just die right away than have to wait for the impact." He shook his head sadly. "The fate of the other six men is unknown. We hope that they made it to the ground, and after that we can only hope they manage to avoid detection and capture."

"My father was captured."

"Your father?"

"He was shot down over France and captured ... He flew Spitfires."

"Ah, that explains your desire to become a pilot."

How did he know that I—

"There was a letter in your file. We'll honour that request, even help you along that path."

"But after tonight I'm not sure I can ever be a pilot. Or even a navigator. I just … just … I don't know how people can do that … you know, come off the plane and talk like nothing happened … just joking around."

"That's the only way they can do it. The only way any of us *can* do it. We get off the plane and we have to put it behind us. There's no point in talking about what just happened, no point in looking back. Instead, you look forward to something, even something silly like a football game, or a night on the town … or breakfast. Do you think you could handle a little grub?"

"Maybe a little."

"Start with toast, dry, and then maybe some cornflakes. Don't even think about bacon or eggs until you've lined your stomach." He smiled. "Come on, kid, time for breakfast."

I stepped out of the pub and into the cold, clean air. It was good to get away from all the smoke, not to mention the noise. After a few pints of beer, men who would never have thought of singing not only started to warble but somehow believed they were the next Frank Sinatra or Bing Crosby. I stayed under the overhang of the building to keep dry, out of the rain.

It had been raining all day. Sometimes it hadn't been much more than a light drizzle, but then it would come down in buckets, which meant our mission for the night had to be cancelled. This was the third night in a row without us going up. The night before, it was the weather over our target that had been stormy, and we were called back just before we got into the planes. The night before that, we'd been halfway across the Channel when a storm had blown over the target and they'd scrubbed the mission and recalled the planes.

Rather than being grateful that they were out of harm's

way for another night, a lot of the men were snarly and upset, and there'd been a number of arguments and a couple of fist fights. I guess there was too much built-up adrenalin, and when it wasn't being used for the mission, it had to get out some other way. I knew the whole thing just left a bad taste in my mouth—unfinished business, as if we hadn't done our job. Tonight wasn't quite as bad because we'd suspected all day that the mission was going to be scrubbed. If we weren't going to finish, it was much better not to have started in the first place.

"Hey, buddy, got a smoke?" It was a soldier, and he had two friends with him. Judging by his accent he was British, but in the darkness it was impossible to make out the unit insignia.

"Sorry, I don't."

"Come on, just one. It's not like I'm asking for the world."

"I don't have any," I repeated.

"Yeah, right, not one … sure," one of the others said.

His words were slurred and I could smell alcohol on him—on them … or was it coming from me? I'd had a couple of pints myself.

"I don't smoke," I said.

I turned and started to walk away, but someone grabbed me and spun me around.

"Bloody air force blokes think they're better than every-body else," one of the soldiers growled.

"I don't think I'm better than anybody," I said.

"You bloody well better not!" he snapped. "Where are you from?"

"Seventy-two squadron."

"Are you being smart with me? Where are you from with that stupid-sounding accent?"

This was looking worse by the second. They stood between me and the entrance to the pub—where there were almost a hundred men from my squadron.

"Hear that, boys? He's too ashamed to tell us where he's from."

All three laughed.

"I'm from Canada."

"Hell, if I was from Canada, I'd be ashamed to admit it too!" he said, and this was followed by more drunken laughter.

"The only shame is that we have to come all the way over here to save you Brits because you're not man enough to take on Hitler by yourselves!" I snapped.

The words were out before I could think of the conse-quences, and almost instantly I regretted them.

"You saying you're more man than us, you little twerp?" one of the soldiers demanded.

Before I could answer or apologize, he pushed me and I almost tumbled over, slipping in the mud before regaining my balance. I backed away slightly as they seemed to fan out and surround me.

"I think the three of us is going to show you who's a man and who ain't!" he said as he pushed me again.

We were now standing in the middle of the muddy lane in the rain. Maybe I could run, or take a swing and run—they were too drunk to catch me. Instead of fists they'd only be able to hurl insults and ... No, I wasn't running from them, not after what I'd been through. I wasn't going to win this fight, but I wasn't going to run away from it either.

I put up my fists. They seemed thrown for a split second, and then all three started to laugh. I was going to make sure I wiped the smirk off the face of the first one. I wouldn't be getting in the last blow, but I was delivering the first one for sure.

"The little fly boy thinks he's man enough to take on the three of us!"

Just then a voice came out of the shadows. "Well, he must be more man than any one of you, if it takes three of you to fight him."

We all turned in the direction of the voice. A man stepped out of the shadows of the building. He was a flyer—a flight lieutenant! And he looked familiar. He was from my squadron.

"Don't let me disturb you," the flight lieutenant said. "I just wanted to have a closer look at what's about to happen."

"We was just having a little fun with 'im," one of the soldiers said. "We wasn't really going to fight him."

"I didn't think you were going to fight. After all, there are only *three* of you. I figured that you'd have to go and find at least another one or two. It usually takes at least four soldiers to take on one flyer ... especially if that flyer is Canadian."

I recognized his accent—or lack of accent, to my ears. He was Canadian too.

"So you boys are really not going to like what's happening next," he continued. "You're going to have to fight two of us. Me and the kid."

"We can't fight you!" one of them exclaimed. "You're an officer. We'd be thrown into the stockade if we fought an officer."

"Then you do have a problem, because I'm going to be fighting you, and it's going to be very one-sided if you don't fight back. Tell you what, don't think of me as an officer, just your superior in every way possible."

All three looked confused now.

"If it'll help, since I am your superior officer, I'm *ordering* you to fight us."

"What?"

"You are hereby *ordered* to engage us in fisticuffs."

"We can't do that," one said, and the other two nodded in agreement. Now they looked more confused than they did drunk ... and they were pretty drunk.

"Are you disobeying a direct order from a superior officer?" he demanded.

"No, sir. I mean, you can't order us around—we're in the army."

"Well, you'd better make up your mind. Either I am your superior officer and you have to obey my order to fight, or I'm not your superior officer and you should feel free to fight us. Which is it? Hurry up, make up your mind! Either way, I see an easy fight in my future!"

They looked at each other, then at the ground, and sort of shuffled their feet in the mud.

"I haven't got all night to stand here in the rain and argue with three army idiots, so what will it be?" He turned to me. "What do *you* think we should do about this?"

I knew at this point all they wanted was the chance to

disappear into the darkness. And with one word, I could let that happen and we could pretend that none of this had happened.

"Well?" he prompted me.

"I don't know about them, sir, but you are definitely *my* superior officer, and you did order a fight ... so ..."

I drew back my fist and popped the mouthy one right in the face, and he tumbled backwards into the mud! There was a second of silence, maybe disbelief, before the second jumped forward and took a swing at me. His fist missed, only brushing my face!

The flight lieutenant jumped forward and connected with a solid shot, and I could almost feel the punch as I heard the crack of his knuckles against the guy's jaw.

Before I could react, the third soldier lunged forward, wrapped his arms around me, and we tumbled over backwards into the mud, him on top of me, his weight forcing the air out of my lungs. I tried to push him off, but he was bigger and heavier. Then the flight lieutenant grabbed him from behind and tackled him into the mud!

I tried to get up, stumbled, fell forward, and connected with the guy, but this time I was on top of him. Our arms were all tangled together and he flailed away, trying to get free. I held on tightly so he couldn't get a good shot, and

I drew back my head and head-butted him in the face! He groaned and instantly stopped fighting. I jumped up. He lay there in the mud, rolling around, his hands covering his face, which was gushing blood. It looked as though I'd broken his nose.

The flight lieutenant was back on his feet and sparring with the other two. He was outnumbered, but he wasn't being outfought. I leaped forward then, bashing into one, who tumbled into the second, and all three of us collapsed in a pile in the mud. Instantly I was yanked to my feet by the flight lieutenant, and the two of us stood overtop of the other two. They didn't seem particularly anxious to get up.

"Get your friend and get out of here or you'll need somebody to carry all three of you!" the flight lieutenant yelled.

They started to get up.

"No!" he yelled. "You crawl over there and get him. You even *try* to get to your feet before that and we'll knock you back down!"

On all fours they crawled through the mud toward their friend, doing their best to keep an eye on us at the same time. When they got to his side, they climbed to their feet and helped him up. He was still clutching his face as if he was afraid his nose might fall off. I felt bad, but not too bad.

Then, one on each side of him, they limped off into the darkness.

"That wasn't exactly what I expected when I stepped outside for a breath of fresh air," the flight lieutenant said.

"Me neither."

"We might want to go back inside before they decide to come back with some friends."

I hadn't even thought of that! I started for the door, but he grabbed me by the arm. "Your cap," he said.

"Oh, yeah." I bent down and picked it up out of the mud. It was filthy!

"You might want to wash that before you put it back on. Come on."

We hurried back into the pub. It was smoky and loud, but warm and dry and, more importantly, safe.

We took a few steps in and noticed that everybody was turning to look at us, and some of them were even pointing. I looked at my tag-team partner. His uniform was covered with mud and his face was filthy. I looked down at my own uniform. No surprise: I looked like a pig that had been wallowing in muck.

The noise died down as some of the men stopped singing and talking and stared at us, obviously wondering what the hell we'd been up to. Some of them were even laughing.

"Can I have your complete attention, please, gentlemen?" the flight lieutenant yelled out, and the room became completely silent. Now every eye *was* on us.

"We had a slight, shall we say, *incident* with three members of the army," he called out. "The kid here settled things nicely. All three ran off with bruised egos, and one with a busted nose!"

There was a huge cheer from the crowd.

"I think we should all raise a glass in his honour in a toast to defeating the enemy—whoever they might be!"

Every man in the place lifted his glass and they cheered even louder! I felt so embarrassed. It looked as though I was going to be the hero of the hour, whether I deserved it or not. I didn't know what to say or do. I just gave a weak little wave and a little smile to go along with it. Who was I to argue with my fellow fly boys?

17

"Time to get up."

"I don't want to get up ... Can't I just sleep a little longer, Mom?"

There was laughter and I suddenly realized why. Not only was I not being woken up by my mother, I wasn't even at home. I opened my eyes. Why was it so bright, and why did my head hurt so badly, and who were these men standing all around my bed? For an instant I thought they were soldiers coming to get me, and then I realized they were all in air force uniforms, and one of them was the flight lieutenant.

"How are you feeling?" he asked.

I tried to sit up and my stomach lurched slightly. "I'm good ... I guess ... except for my head. I must have gotten hit harder than I thought."

"The only thing you got hit with came out of a bottle. You were really slugging it back last night."

It all came back to me in a rush. People had kept on

coming over, offering congratulations, a slap on the back, or a handshake, and most of them bought me a drink. I couldn't remember how many drinks I'd had. I couldn't even remember the end of the night.

"I guess I had a little too much to drink."

"You passed 'a little too much' a little bit before midnight. You probably have a hangover," the flight lieutenant said.

"I think it would have hurt less if somebody had actually hit me with the bottle instead of letting me drink what was inside," I groaned. That was apparently pretty funny, because it made them all laugh.

"Have you never had a hangover before?" one of the other men asked. He had what I'd come to recognize as an Australian accent.

I started to shake my head, but that made it hurt even more. "No, never," I said softly.

The flight lieutenant leaned over my bed. "So, you're probably wondering why you're waking up with a flight crew standing over you."

"I *was* wondering ... but I was just glad it wasn't a bunch of army grunts."

They laughed again, and the loudness hurt my head.

"Do you remember any of us?" he asked.

I looked around from face to face. They all smiled and

they did look familiar … but I certainly didn't remember any of them by name.

I shook my head. "I don't remember much of last night."

"You do remember me, don't you?"

I nodded. His name was Blackburn … I thought maybe Jed was his first name.

"The fight I remember. Being told it was rude to turn down a drink I remember. After that …" I shrugged.

"I guess you remember the important parts, Davie."

For a split second I almost didn't remember I was Davie.

"You might be wondering why my crew and I are in here," he said.

"My head is hurting too much to wonder much … But yeah, why are you here?"

"I just came from the CO. I asked and he agreed to assign you to be my navigator. That is, if you're willing to be assigned to my crew."

That kind of woke me up! "Of course … if he thinks I'm ready."

"He said you were ready."

I'd been out on five missions, and on the last three I had done all the mapping and charting. Mike had just sat back and watched.

"I hope I'm ready, sir."

"The first thing you have to know is that we're pretty informal on this crew. It's Jed, not sir. Second, maybe you'd better get to know the members of my crew when you're sober enough to actually remember who they are. Sometimes I feel more like a zookeeper than a pilot."

Three of them suddenly started to make animal noises. One was barking like a dog, another imitated some sort of jungle bird, and the third was mooing.

"I said zookeeper, not farmer," Jed said to the man who was mooing.

"When I was growing up, we was so poor that my papa would take us to a barn and tell us that we *was* at a zoo," the man who had been mooing replied.

"You can see that our maturity level is somewhat questionable. Join us for breakfast and we'll talk about everything."

I started to get up and stopped. I really didn't need an audience to watch me dress. "Can I have a little privacy?"

"You can, but first we have to tell you how to get dressed," another one of the crew replied with a thick Australian accent.

"I don't understand ... I know how to get dressed."

"But you probably don't know the *right* way," he replied, and they all laughed.

I was quickly going from confused to worried.

"To be part of this crew, you have to do everything *right*."

"I always try to do that."

"Not try, mate, *succeed*. Everything has to be *right*. Everybody on our crew always puts on their pants right leg first."

"And then your shirt, right arm in the right sleeve first," another man added.

"And then you put on your right sock and right shoe before either left sock or shoe goes on. Do you understand?"

"Sure. You like things to go in a certain order."

"An *exact* order. We believe if we all do it the same way, it protects us from harm."

The fact that I *did* understand showed that I'd been here too long already. I had quickly learned that men in the air force were just about the most superstitious people in the world. Almost everybody had a lucky charm or a superstition, or needed to do things in exactly the same order or eat exactly the same food before every mission. Part of it was just plain crazy, but in other ways it was ordinary human nature—trying to get control over something because there was so much that was beyond your control.

"Okay, I understand. *Now* can I have some privacy?"

"Come on, lads, let's leave him to get dressed," Jed said, and they all filed out of the room—making more animal noises as they left.

I climbed out of bed. I was already in my skivvies and undershirt. I grabbed my pants and went to slip them on and stopped: I had put my left leg in first. I pulled it back out and went right leg first. I finished putting them on and then grabbed my shirt—right arm first. Next, right sock and shoe, left sock and shoe, and I finished with my jacket—of course putting my right arm in first. I wondered if I should wash the right side of my face first and brush the teeth on the right side of my mouth first. I decided not to do either until after breakfast, and after I'd asked them about those important procedures.

The mess hall was packed and noisy, a little steamy, and it smelled of breakfast. This morning, that smell was not only unappealing, it actually made me feel a bit nauseous. I looked all around. There they were, at a table in the far corner.

"Hey, Davie!" one of them yelled, and three of them waved. I waved back and went over.

"Here, take a seat," one of them offered, pulling it out.

"And drink this," a second said as he pushed a mug in front of me.

"Thanks."

I took a sip and gagged and coughed as it went down the wrong way. One of them slapped me on the back.

"What is this?" I asked, holding the mug up.

"Strong tea and a little hair of the dog."

"What does that mean?"

"Best thing for a hangover is a little bit of the hair from the dog that bit you," Jed said. "There's a wee bit of whisky in there. It'll help your head."

"Really?"

"He knows what he's talking about," one of the others said. "He can vouch for that from experience."

"In *his* case, lots of experience!" another of the crew chimed in, and they all laughed. "You'll see for yourself once you're part of our crew."

"But before you make that decision," Jed said, "there's one more thing you need to know: we're part of the pathfinders group."

"Pathfinders!"

One of them pointed to the little patch on his shoulder. The pathfinders were the crews that went in first to mark the target for the main bomber group.

"But I don't have that much experience as a navigator," I said.

"We heard you're a natural."

"But if I don't plot the perfect course, the whole mission would go wrong."

"Not to worry," Jed said. "That part of the job generally falls to the finders—the first planes in, which drop flares. We're the second group, the markers. We follow closely behind the planes that do the very initial drop of flares, and we lay down incendiary bombs to really light the place up for the main bomber group."

"You just have to get us close, and then I look for those flares," one of the men said. "Then it's bombs away."

"And we do fly in a formation of between three and six planes, so you will have some additional help to locate the flares," Jed said. "Some people think our job is more dangerous than the others, but I don't agree. It's true that we come in at a lower altitude and with a much smaller formation, but generally the ack-ack fire is less because they don't have as much time to get ready for us, and by the time they do scramble fighter planes, we're already away from the target."

"I was just wondering—your last navigator … did he … die?"

"He finished his tour and was sent home," Jed explained. "So, are you in?"

I stood up. "McWilliams, David, navigator, reporting for duty—" I almost said *sir* but then remembered. "Reporting for duty, *Jed*."

18

"Letter from home?"

I looked up from my bunk. It was Jacko, the wireless operator for my crew.

"It's from my best friend, Chip."

"He didn't enlist?"

"He's not—" I almost said he wasn't old enough. "He's not through his school year. He failed a grade, but come June he's going to enlist for sure."

"Good to hear it. Nothing worse than a bunch of idiots and cowards sitting at home. Hardest part is they just don't know what we're going through. They watch those newsreels and read the papers and they think they know what it's like."

"They couldn't. Nobody could if they weren't here. I'm here and I still don't believe it sometimes."

"I thought that was just me!" he said and laughed. "Anyhoo, enough of reality. I'm heading down to the town for a pint in the pub. Do you want to come along?"

"I'd better write back."

"Now you're just making me feel guilty. I owe a letter to my parents, and all three of my girlfriends."

"*Three?*"

"Well, those are the three back home. You wouldn't expect me to write to the two here in town when I can just pop in and see them any time I want." He laughed again. "I'll hoist an extra pint for you when I'm down there."

"Please, do that."

I hadn't had anything to drink—not even a sip—for two weeks. Not since that eventful evening. I figured there was a chance I was never going to drink again after that.

I ran my finger down the page, looking for the spot where I'd stopped reading. There it was.

We've already had snow—twice—but so far it hasn't stayed on the ground. You may want to mention something to your mother about the unseasonably cold weather. I'm sure the weather is better in England ... well, at least warmer, but I imagine wet and foggy.

I have some good news: I've been assigned to the mailroom for the remainder of the school year. Old man Beamish told me how "disappointed" he was in me since I'd shown "so much promise" this year. Apparently he was convinced that you were

*the only impediment to my becoming the headmaster's prize
pet.*

*For what it's worth, it's not nearly the same here without
you. Not nearly as much fun. I can only imagine the good times
you're having and I want you to promise me that you'll save me
at least a little piece of the war. Remember, no fair winning it
before I've had a chance to get into the action! Save some of the
fun for me!*

I shook my head slowly. Fun ... was that what I was
having? Going up in a plane and having people shoot at me,
trying to kill me, while I dropped bombs on them, trying
to kill them. Getting to know men, not knowing if or when
they might die, but knowing that each night, each mission,
would be the end of somebody's life, that it *could* be the end
of my life. Yes, this was *such* fun.

Here I was, only seventeen, but each night I was as close
to death as a ninety-year-old man. No, closer. How could I
tell that to Chip? What could I write? What *should* I write? I
went back to his letter.

*I've started to write home to my mother to tell her about all the
people who are sick at school. You know our mothers talk, so I'm
helping to set the stage for "somebody" to get pneumonia and not*

be able to go home over Christmas. In the meantime, you just
keep yourself well and healthy. I'm going to need a good pilot in
about ten months, so get your wings before I get there!

> *All the best—your best friend,*
> *Chip*

I set his letter down. I'd been putting off writing. I
needed to write something to my mother, and to Chip. I
picked up a pen.

Dear Chip,

Thank you so much for your letter and for all your support—
both for what I'm doing over here but also what you're doing
back home to make it all possible. It's all pretty exciting over here.
Since my last letter I've been assigned to a full-time crew as their
navigator. They're a bunch of great guys, from all over the world.

Both the wireless operator—Jacko—and the bomb aimer—
Drew—are from Australia. They're a little on the crazy side,
which is to say they remind me of you! Our flight engineer—
Scottie—is a Kiwi. Funny how New Zealand and Australia
are so close together but the people are so different. Somebody
told me that the Australians are more like the Americans
and the Kiwis are like Canadians. Scottie is very calm, even
when all hell is breaking loose around us. Our tail gunner—

Sandy—is from England, and the top gunner—Glen—is
an American. He's been on more missions than anybody in
the whole squadron. He volunteered to fight the Nazis two
years before the U.S. got into the war. Surprisingly both of the
gunners are smaller than me! It's a real advantage to be small
when you're wedging into a turret! And though they may be
small, they're both scrappy. If somebody bothers one of them, he
has to fight both of them. Actually if anybody bothers anybody
on the crew, they have to fight all of us. Finally there's our
skipper. He's Canadian and from B.C. He's married and has a
kid almost my age. He's a good pilot, and I'm lucky to be flying
with him because he keeps the whole thing going.

So far I've been with them for six missions. Combine that with
the five missions I did in training and I'm almost one-third of
the way to being finished my tour of duty. If you don't hurry up,
I'll be gone before you get here!

I looked down at the words I'd written. Those were all
the things I was supposed to write, and while none of it was
a lie, I wasn't really writing what I felt. Maybe I owed Chip
more than that.

I know this all sounds pretty glamorous, but I think about being
back in school a lot. I never thought I'd miss my old school, old

friends, and even old man Beamish so much. Please be sure to give him a hug and a kiss on the top of his bald head for me the next time you see him. That should either result in you being permanently transferred to the mailroom or being made the class valedictorian.

I do miss having you around—you are my best friend. I'd like to say that I wish you were here, but I'm so glad that you're not. I know this seems romantic and exciting from a distance. That's how I saw it. And it is exciting—if excitement means not knowing if you're going to live or die from day to day. People do die. Not just people, but people I've known, people who have become my friends. I'll never forget the last conversation I had with the first man I knew who died. I'll never forget his face.

I'm not saying that I'm sorry I did what I did to enlist. I know that what I'm doing—what we're all doing—is important. We are fighting against an evil that needs to be defeated. I'm prepared for what may happen, but I don't want this for you or anybody else. I'm here to do my job, to try to end things as soon as we can so that you won't have to come over here. Nothing would make me happier than to have this over before you get a chance to enlist. Actually that's wrong—nothing would make me happier than to have it end today. I'm sorry if I sound like a killjoy, and I hope you understand.

I know I've already asked a lot from you, but I'd like to ask *for one more favour. If something happens to me, I want you to promise not to blame yourself for helping me. This was my idea. You are my best friend, probably the best friend I'll ever have if I live to be ninety, and maybe that's why I'm so glad that you're over there and not here.*

Time passes so strangely here. It seems impossible to believe that it was only a few months ago I left. Sometimes it seems like three years and sometimes it feels like another lifetime ago. I guess in some ways, it is another lifetime ago.

This is the last letter you'll get from me before Christmas, so I wish you a very happy Christmas and all the best in the coming New Year.

> *Your good friend,*
> *Davie*

I had one more thing to add, something that would explain the letter I was enclosing for my mother, just in case the censor got suspicious.

P.S. Somehow when my brother Robbie sent me his last letter, it mistakenly included a letter he intended to send to our mother. I've enclosed it—could you please give it to him to forward to her?

19

The plane banked sharply to starboard as Jed responded to my latest course correction. I knew without looking that the other planes would be following our change, but I got up to look anyway, holding on to the table as I stood. I looked out of the canopy to the sides and behind, and I could make out the darkened outlines of the other five planes in our formation. The plane levelled out. We were going to come in over the target travelling east to west; the finders had come in north to south, and we wanted to confuse the gunners who would be throwing flak our way.

"What's our altitude?" Jed asked.

His voice, as usual, was calm, and that always made me feel calmer. He wasn't just our pilot, he was like everybody's older brother—or in my case, like a father.

"Forty-two hundred feet," Scottie replied, looking at the instruments.

"I'm going to drop down another three hundred feet."

"Drop down a few more and we can shake hands with the ack-ack gunners," Scottie joked.

"I heard the gunners are all female, so maybe a pretty Fräulein would give me a little kiss," Jacko chipped in.

"That would be fraternizing with the enemy," Jed said. "Although it's probably better to be kissed by their lips than by their flak!"

The anti-aircraft shells were set with a proximity fuse to go off at a certain altitude. It was probably a pretty safe bet that nobody would set them to explode at *under* four thousand feet. We could still get hit, even have a shell go in the bottom and come out through the top, but it wouldn't explode. That made it only slightly less dangerous and deadly.

"Any sign of flares, Drew?"

From his perch in the nose cone, he had the best view of the ground below. "Nothing yet, Skip."

"We're still three miles from the target," I answered— wondering if they were doubting my course correction.

"Nobody is questioning that we're on target," Jed said, putting my unspoken concerns to rest. He was always able to say the right thing.

"Wait!" Drew cried out. "I'm seeing some flares just off to port ... What are tonight's colours?"

"They dropped pink pansies," Jacko called from the wireless station. "Look for pink pansies."

"Are they pink?" Jed asked.

"No, I don't think so. White, definitely not pink … They must be decoys."

The Germans would put out their own flares to try to confuse us—make us think that the target was someplace else so we'd drop our bombs and then cause the whole squadron to miss the mark as well, dropping on the false target that we'd marked. The bombers coming in at nineteen thousand feet in the dark couldn't possibly see the ground. They looked for fire—the result of our incendiary bombs—and dropped their loads right on top of that.

"There they are!" Drew called out. "Straight ahead."

I looked past Jed and Scottie, through the front of the canopy. There before us were pink pansies, a few scattered in a line and then hundreds of bright pink flares. Down below on the ground I knew there were German soldiers desperately scrambling around trying to extinguish them before we could use them for our mark. It was too late. They weren't going to see what hit them.

"Opening bomb doors," Scottie said.

I listened for the hydraulics.

"Sixty seconds," Drew said. "Correct three degrees starboard."

"Roger that, will release the bombs on your mark," Jed said. "We're staying low and level."

"Where the heck is all the flak?" Jacko asked.

Almost as if the gunners on the ground had heard his question, there was a series of explosions and the sky lit up! Bright searchlights started sweeping the sky, looking for us.

"You happy now, mate?" Jacko asked.

"I'd be happier if I was sitting beside a fine young Sheila."

"They can both be deadly."

"Everybody off the com except Drew," Jed said.

The flak was well off to the side and above our position. They were lighting up the sky on the same course that the finders had taken; they'd heard our engines but expected us to come in from the same direction. They'd correct that quickly.

"Ten seconds," Drew said. "Keep it level if you can."

We were almost over the target. I looked down through Scottie's feet into the bubble that contained Drew. His darkened silhouette was visible, and beneath him I could see some of the pink pansies. We were coming right over them.

There was a thunderous crash that made the plane shake

and bounce, and the whole sky lit up so brightly that my eyes lost focus for a second.

"Hold her steady, will you, Skipper?" Drew called out. "Releasing in three … two … now!"

"Bombs away, bombs away!" Scottie yelled.

I felt the bombs drop and then we shot upward! We were suddenly surrounded by light, and flak was exploding just over our heads. They'd adjusted the timers but not enough—we were still beneath the explosions.

"Flak to the port! Hard to starboard!" Drew shouted.

Almost instantly we banked hard to the right and dropped down even farther to gain speed and defy the gunners. I looked out through the canopy. We'd banked so hard that I could make out the ground below and saw the first bombs hit! The entire area lit up brightly. Below was a rail yard filled with freight cars and locomotives, and I could see that some of them were already ablaze. Beyond them were small houses and a gigantic cathedral, and from this height I could see that the steeple was in ruins. And then I saw the river and the bend that showed on my maps. That was the bearing I'd use for the next mark.

We flattened out, but we were still descending, using gravity to increase our speed. The faster we could get away, the better the chance of avoiding enemy fighters—or at least avoiding them for longer.

"Wow, you should see it from here!" our tail gunner yelled out. "We really lit it up down there ... It looks like a barbecue!"

"Then we did our job well."

"Give me a new heading, please, Davie," Jed asked.

"Change course to northeast, twenty-two degrees."

"Are you taking us home or to Berlin?" Scottie asked.

"Have faith. If you don't expect it, neither will they."

"Okay, everybody, follow my bearing. Tighten up and expect action," Jed ordered.

I looked out through the canopy. On the port were two planes, but where were the other three? I scanned the sky, looking for a visual, but couldn't see anybody else. The Lancasters were big but the sky was bigger, and in the dark it was easy to get lost.

"Jacko, where is everybody?" I asked. "Are they following?"

"I'm getting readings from four other planes."

"Four?" Jed asked. "Where's the fifth?"

"Sorry, Skip, it took fire, there were flames ... I saw it go down," Glen said.

"Did you see chutes? Did you see anybody get out?" Jed asked.

"I didn't see anybody, but when you banked, I lost sight. They could have bailed."

I knew—everybody knew—that at this altitude you only had seconds to get out, and if that didn't happen you were going to go down in the plane. I pictured the Lancaster spiralling down and the crew scrambling to get on their chutes, fighting against gravity and the force of the plane, desperately trying to get to the emergency hatches before … before it was too late.

"We got company coming!" Jacko yelled out. "Ten, maybe twelve blips showing on the fishpond. Coming too fast to be anything but fighters."

"Any visuals from anybody?" Jed asked.

"You won't see anything yet," Jacko said. "They're still over two miles away. High, maybe seven thousand feet to the southeast … not on an intercept course … at least not yet."

"Let's make it harder for them to find us," Jed said.

The plane dipped and we descended even more. I grabbed on to the table and pulled myself down until I was wedged underneath.

"We're slightly over two thousand feet," Scottie said.

"Tell me when we get to fifteen hundred."

"I'll give you readings every hundred feet in case you decide to level out before that," Scottie replied.

I guess that was his way of saying he would have preferred a little more altitude. Jed had used this technique before. Dropping down not only gained speed but made it difficult for us to be tracked by radar. As well, if we did encounter fighters, they would always be coming from above, where we at least had a gunner.

There were advantages to the strategy, but there was also one terrible danger. At this low altitude, there was almost no time to bail out if there was a problem. Parachutes needed at least five hundred feet to be effective, and there would be only a few seconds before we dropped to that height. I reached out with my foot and hooked my parachute and pulled it toward me until I could grab it with my hand.

"Where are the bandits?" Jed asked.

"They're circling back, waiting for the main formation."

I felt a wave of relief wash over my entire body. We were safe. At least, safer for a few more minutes. But this was no time to relax. I pulled the blackout curtain and turned on the little reading light. It was almost time for another course correction.

20

The sun peeked over the horizon, and from behind us came a warm glow that lit up the canopy.

"It appears that we've lived to fight another day," Jed said. "That is one beautiful sunrise!"

"Any sunrise you're alive to see is a beautiful one!" Glen replied. He had left the top gun turret and was standing beside me in the canopy, right behind Jed and Scottie.

"You boys know that the most beautiful sunrises in the world are in Australia. And that doesn't seem fair since we already have the most beautiful women as well!" Jacko added over the intercom.

"And the most boastful men!" Scottie said.

"Pure jealousy from a man whose country has more sheep than women!" Jacko yelled.

"Compared to some of your Aussie women, the New Zealand sheep look mighty pretty."

"Spoken like a true Kiwi. And we're not boasting. It's just the facts—nothing but the facts!" Drew added from the nose cone of the plane.

I didn't want to get caught in another battle between the Kiwi and the Aussies, but I thought they were both wrong. I didn't know about the women, but I knew the best sunrises were in Ontario.

In the morning light I could clearly see the rest of the Lancs in our formation. I only wished there were six planes in the formation, not five. I'd avoided asking which plane was missing—which men. I could have found out by looking at the numbers on the sides, but I didn't look. What did it matter? Whichever plane had gone down contained seven men I knew. Each plane held at least one person I called a friend.

Instead, I looked out at our escort. For the last hour we'd been accompanied by a formation of six Spitfires. They were spread out, above and off to the port side, there to provide support, watching for enemy aircraft. Their appearance was almost a guarantee that no fighters were going to try to attack. We were as good as home, and that was why Glen could come out of the gun turret. We were being watched and protected by the Spits now.

Those Spitfires were beautiful beyond words. They were

graceful, nimble, and so agile. I still dreamed about piloting one of them, but I'd been thinking more and more lately about taking the controls of a Lancaster.

Then there were the times I just thought about flying nothing, finishing my tour and going home. I missed so much about being there. Not just the people, but the smell of the air, even the snow and cold. The closest I got to Canadian winter weather was being up in the Lancaster, the temperature so low that my fingers got numb. But up there the shaking was only partially because of the cold. I was still afraid every time I went up.

Jed had said that anybody who *wasn't* afraid shouldn't even go up because he was obviously too crazy for combat. Of course, that wasn't just a joke. Some men did crack up. They were so afraid that they couldn't go up anymore; they just couldn't do it.

Two weeks ago, one of the pilots had been forced to abort his mission and circle back for a landing because his flight engineer had "lost it." He started screaming and yelling about how he knew they were all going to die on that mission. They'd tried to calm him down, but he just got worse and worse, and finally they had to restrain him because he was trying to get into his parachute and jump. Once they landed, they took him away to see the medical officer. They said he was given medication and then taken to a hospital for "rest."

The thing was, that mission had been particularly deadly. Four planes from our squadron hadn't come back. Maybe he really did know something, and by doing what he did he'd saved his own life and the lives of the members of his crew.

I knew it was strange even to think that way, but what with all the superstitions and things that we all did, who was to say who else was crazy? How crazy was it to climb into an airplane and drop bombs on people while they tried to blow you out of the sky?

I looked up and saw in the distance the glimmer of the Channel. Underneath us—about eight thousand feet below—was the French countryside. From our height it was all so calm and beautiful that it almost took my breath away. There was no hint of the war that was taking place down there, no signs of destruction, or of soldiers or tanks or anything related to war … So peaceful looking. Of course, from far enough away, appearances could be deceiving— the same way that looking at the war from North America was so different from seeing it up close.

We'd be back at base and eating breakfast in less than sixty minutes. I could almost smell the bacon and eggs. I was hungry. The food always tasted so good after a mission. In fact, everything seemed different after a mission. As bizarre as it sounded, somehow even colours looked brighter. I wasn't sure if it was because our senses were still working full time to keep us alive or simply that we were so grateful we *were* still alive.

"Davie," Jed called out, "are you ready for a little time behind the yoke?"

"Always ready!"

Most types of bombers had a pilot and a co-pilot, so if something happened to the pilot there was still somebody to fly the plane. But the Lancaster had only the one pilot. They'd found that if a pilot was hit by flak or strafed by machine-gun fire, in most cases the co-pilot was killed as well. So they figured, why waste a second pilot?

With the Lancs they had a policy of giving other members of the crew some supervised time behind the yoke, just in case there ever was a time when the pilot was disabled. That usually involved splitting time among the flight engineer, the navigator, and the wireless operator. But ever since they'd found out I was hoping to become a pilot, I'd taken most of the time. In fact, Jed had made sure there was extra time, and he'd also spent hours and hours with me on the ground, either in the mess hall or in the cockpit, teaching me all about the Lancaster. I did know how to fly this plane ... well, if flying it didn't include taking off or landing, or changing directions too fast or sharply, or taking evasive action or ... I guess you might say I could fly it a little.

Jed slid to one side and I slipped in beside him, first getting my feet on the rudder pedal and then taking the yoke. I still felt my palms get all moist. I was nervous, but nothing like the first few times I'd sat behind the controls. I was more frightened to take the stick then than I'd been when they were hurling flak up at us and it was exploding all around the plane. At least if we'd all died then, it wouldn't have been because I'd screwed up.

Jed got up and stood behind me. The controls were all mine. I pushed the yoke forward and the plane responded, dipping a bit. I always did that when I first started flying because I liked to have the feel of the plane, to make it respond to my hands on the controls. I pulled the stick back ever so slightly to level it off again.

The Lancaster was what they called a muscle plane. The yoke and the rudders were manual and working them required serious muscle. You could often tell a Lancaster pilot by the way his arms were developed. Eight hours behind the yoke was really hard work, almost like lifting weights. I knew that after fifteen or twenty minutes, I would start to feel it in my arms.

I glanced over at Scottie. He was sitting there monitoring his instruments. He looked very relaxed. I was glad that he felt comfortable enough with my flying to be relaxed. Or at least if he *wasn't* confident, he was kind enough not to show it.

"Squadron leader, this is Spitfire leader," came a call over the radio.

I looked over my shoulder for Jed. I didn't see him. I turned the other way. He wasn't there either.

"He's in the back, talking to Sandy," Scottie said.

"Can you go and get him?"

"Why?"

"They want to talk to the squadron leader!"

"When you're in that seat, you're the squadron leader. Ask them what they want."

"This is Spitfire leader to squadron leader," the voice called out again. "Do you read me?"

At that same instant a Spitfire appeared just off our starboard side. He was close enough that I could see his face.

"Answer him," Scottie said.

"Um ... hello ... Spitfire leader ... I hear you." I deliberately didn't identify myself as the squadron leader.

"We're about to break off our escort. You're home free from this point," he said.

"Okay, sure, thanks for your help," I replied.

"It was our pleasure." He gave me a thumbs-up. I waved back and he waggled his wings and then banked sharply and disappeared beneath us. The other Spitfires broke off their escorts too, dipping, climbing, and banking, leaving us.

"I guess we're on our own," I said, "which means we should probably have our top gunner back in his turret."

"We're almost home," Glen replied.

"Better do what the skipper wants," Scottie said. "You might outrank him, but as long as he's in the captain's seat, he's in charge."

"Yes, sir, Captain McWilliams, sir!" Glen said.

I couldn't help but laugh, but I kept my attention on the job of flying. I listened for the engines, turning my head first one way and then the other. There was a slightly different tone coming from the port side ... at least I thought there was. I looked at the engines. There was nothing visible, certainly no smoke or fumes.

"Scottie, can you check the port engines? Is something happening with one of them?"

"No need to check. The outside port engine is running rough. I suspect that one of the propellers is damaged."

"Damaged?"

"Probably took a piece of flak. I won't be able to tell until we land, unless I turn off the engine now … Do you want me to do that?"

"I'm not that curious."

"We could fly with two engines if we needed to," Scottie said.

"Let's hope we never need to."

The white cliffs of Dover were looming on the horizon. I looked for one particular cliff—it had a peculiar coloration pattern—as my marker. From this altitude and in daylight, I could find our way home simply by landmarks, so there was no need for me to navigate a course. From the pilot's seat I could do it all visually.

I banked slightly to one side to correct my course. The other planes in the formation responded similarly. I wasn't just piloting us home, I was directing the entire formation. Unbelievably here I was behind the yoke of a Lancaster bomber having come back from a bombing mission over Germany, while what I should have been doing was trying to finish high school. I wished my mother and father could know about what I was doing. They'd be so proud of me … Or no, they wouldn't. They'd be worried and upset and mad as hell. And who could blame them?

21

"Davie, are you in there?" Jed asked.

I started slightly. "I'm here," I said quietly, hidden in the darkness. I brushed away the tears with the back of my hand. I was so grateful for the darkness, and for the fact that I didn't have to share a room now.

"Were you sleeping?"

"Not sleeping, just resting my eyes a little." I was trying to make my voice sound normal, but it wasn't quite right.

"Being up all night can really play havoc with your sleeping schedule. Are you coming for dinner? They've done up a nice roast for Christmas Eve."

"In a bit."

"Don't leave it too long or there'll be nothing left. You know the boys can eat."

"I won't be long." My voice definitely sounded off.

"You know, Davie, it's better to be with other people than by yourself at times like this." Jed took a step into my room. "Mind if I turn on the light?"

"Sure ... of course."

The light came on, catching me wiping my eyes again, and I tried to pretend I was just shielding them from the brightness.

He took the chair from my desk, spun it around, put it down right in front of me, and sat on it backwards.

"How are you doing?" he asked.

I shrugged. "I've been better."

"It's hard to be away from your family any time, but Christmas is the hardest."

"It is hard." I sat up on the edge of my bed.

"I don't mind telling you, I've shed a few tears today," he said.

"Really?"

"It's not a sign of weakness, you know, just caring. You've been crying?"

"A bit," I admitted.

"It's natural. I know I miss my wife and son tremendously. This is my third Christmas away from them."

"That's rough ... rougher, I guess ... It's not like I have a wife or kids."

"You'd better *not* have kids yet!" He laughed. "But I'm sure you must be missing your family."

I nodded my head. "A lot."

"Who's at home?"

"I have a younger brother and two little sisters, and of course my mom."

"It must be pretty hard on all of them, what with you and your father both being gone."

"This is his third Christmas away too. I know how much harder he has it than me, so I shouldn't be complaining."

"We all know there's no point in complaining ... Stiff upper lip, as the English say."

I was a bit guilty about feeling so sorry for myself—lots of people were far worse off—

"But you know, we're not English," Jed said. "And it takes a strong man to realize that he might not be so strong *all* the time. You have a right to feel a bit blue. You know what made me feel better today ... well, a little better?"

"What?"

"I just finished writing home. I try to write to them as though they're right here in the room with me and we're just having a little talk. When was the last time you wrote home?"

"A week or so ago."

"Maybe it's time to start a letter. I bet your mother would really like to hear from you."

I nodded.

"It'll make it seem like they're closer." He got up and put a hand on my shoulder. "You're a good kid. I'd be proud to have you as my son."

I felt the same about him—as if he was kind of a second father. He was more than my pilot, my crew member. He'd been there to take care of me from that first night outside the pub.

"I'll make sure to save you a good piece of roast beef and some Yorkshire pudding."

"Thanks."

"But I've got to be honest with you—if you take too long, I may eat your pudding myself. After supper a few of us are heading into town for a Christmas Eve service. Are you going to come along?"

"I'd like that. If I was home, we'd be going to church."

Jed smiled and left the room. I got off my bed and brought the chair back over to the desk and sat down.

I'd write, but I wasn't sure what to write about. It was different for Jed—he could tell his family what he was doing, what his days were like, talk to them as though they were sitting right there with him. There was no way I could write a letter like that, because my mother didn't even know I was here.

Instead, I'd have to make up things about being in school,

and how I was getting over the pneumonia that had kept me from coming home over Christmas. It would give her some comfort, but how was it going to make me feel better to write her a bunch of lies? Maybe it was time I told the truth.

I pulled a pen and some writing paper out of the desk drawer.

Dearest Mother,

I am writing to you on Christmas Eve—my first Christmas apart from my family. I know that this must be as hard for you as it is for me. I'm feeling a great weight of sadness. This is not simply because I miss my beloved family, but also because I feel tremendous guilt over the manner in which I've deceived you and everybody else. I'll try to explain my actions as best I can.

I clearly remember the reasons behind my decision—although they have such a dreamlike innocence to them when I think of them now. I felt that I had an obligation to serve—for King and Country—to help stop the Nazis. I believed in the just cause of this war and that we needed to defeat our enemies.

It was also, very much, a personal decision. I think in the back of my head, I believed that by coming over here not only could I be closer to Father, but I might also, by my involvement, help to bring him home sooner. I know, in hindsight, that this thinking might seem rather juvenile—and in fact many of the thoughts and beliefs that brought me here could be described as those of a silly boy.

My decision was made in a rush of youthful exuberance. It was all a sort of game—a game in which I would need to fool everybody so I could be shipped overseas—and beyond that, the war itself, from afar, I saw as simply glamorous and exciting. The danger I imagined was abstract and merely added to the excitement. The only threat I could imagine was to our German enemies. I could not conceive of dying, or being injured in any way. I felt invincible.

While I have been gone slightly less than four months, I feel that many of these immature and juvenile thoughts have left me. I am no longer a boy. I feel so much older. I think about things I would never have dreamed of before. I spend time contemplating life and death and the meaning of both. Death is in my thoughts because it is my constant companion.

As strange as it may sound, this has made me appreciate life more than I ever did before. I think I took things for granted—a beautiful sunrise, the support of a friend, and the love of my family. Perhaps when everything can be lost in the next few moments or days, you truly learn to value what you have.

I know this is not a game. This is not play. This is deadly serious. Lives are taken and lost. I have seen people I know die. I can't really know of the deaths that have taken place below

as a result of my actions, but I have seen the devastation that
we cause. I console myself by hoping and praying that it is only
enemy soldiers who have perished——although I know that they
too have mothers and wives and children who love them. In all
likelihood some of those innocents have also perished by our
actions.

Sometimes I think about what my life would be like if I had
never started along this path. I have thought about——really fanta-
sized about——simply snapping my fingers and undoing all that I
have done, waking up in a bed back home. Then I realize that even
if I had that magical power, I would not be able to use it. I have set
out upon a course and must follow it to the end. I cannot abandon
my friends and my crew mates. This is my place. This is my life. I am
part of something important, vital, and necessary. We are fighting
against a terrible evil, and this is now my place.

If you receive this letter, it is because I am not coming home,
because I have been killed or captured. I need you to know how
much I love you. You have been the best mother a boy could
ever have and I beg your forgiveness for the sadness I will have
caused.

> With great love,
> Your son,
> Robert

I took the letter, folded it, and slipped it into an envelope. I sealed it and wrote my mother's name across the front and then added, *Please send to my mother in the event of my death or capture*, and placed it back in the drawer.

It was done, and it did make me feel a little bit better. At least she'd know the reasons why I'd done this and she wouldn't blame herself.

I left my room and heard voices—singing. As I hurried down the hall, the voices got louder and stronger. I stopped at the door of the mess hall, stunned. The lights were out and the whole room was filled with candles, and all of the men, hundreds and hundreds, were on their feet, singing "Silent Night." Many of them were standing with their heads bowed. Others were holding hands and swaying ever so slightly to the music. The singing was simply beautiful. I stepped into the room and joined in the song.

> *Silent night, holy night,*
> *All is calm, all is bright,*
> *Round yon Virgin Mother and Child,*
> *Holy infant so tender and mild,*
> *Sleep in heavenly peace,*
> *Sleep in heavenly peace.*

My voice caught and I knew I was going to start to cry. I tried to choke back the tears, but I noticed that all around me men were crying. So I let the tears flow. I didn't know if I could have stopped them even if I'd tried.

22

I stomped my feet and rubbed my hands together to try to drive away the cold. We hadn't even got up to cruising altitude yet, but the plane was already freezing. We'd been told that it had snowed last night—not at our base in England but in the territory we'd be flying over—and thank goodness the cloud cover still remained. Nobody wanted to fly in a storm, but clouds gave us someplace to hide from enemy aircraft and gunners on the ground.

Below us, the French countryside—invisible from this height and in the darkness—was supposedly coated in a fresh layer of white. I imagined it must look very pretty, with most of the visible destruction of war covered up. I used to think that someday I'd come back and see it—either after France had been liberated or maybe even later, long after the war was over. Right now, though, I was happy to have a lot of distance between me and the ground.

It was wet and drab back at our base—typical English wintertime weather. No snow, just lots of rain and drizzle that turned the earth into grey, grimy mud. It just didn't seem like Christmas without snow. There was almost always snow on the ground back home at this time of year, and I couldn't help picturing what their Christmas morning must have been like: fresh white snow, smoke rising from the chimney, the house all decorated, and us sitting around the Christmas tree, sipping hot apple cider, taking turns opening presents, my brother and sisters squabbling … Even that would have been music to my ears.

"Davie, do you have that course change plotted?" Jed asked over the intercom.

"Got it plotted. Stay the course for another"—I looked at my watch—"eight minutes."

"Good, just making sure you're still awake back there."

"I'm awake."

"I don't want any of you falling asleep," Jed said.

"That would be almost impossible with all this chattering going on," Jacko replied. "Could we at least talk quietly? My head feels like it's going to split in two."

"A little too much celebration?" Jed replied.

"A *lot* too much celebration. That's what happens when they give us a couple of days off."

We hadn't flown a mission on either Christmas Eve or, technically, Christmas Day. It was a small respite from the war for both us and the people on the ground. It was sort of odd and sweet all at once—taking a day off from war to honour the Prince of Peace.

It had been three in the morning on December 26 by the time we got in our planes and up into the air. We'd been delayed partially by the storm on our route, but it was also a late-start mission. Missions were flown at different times, often the later the better, because the gunners below went to sleep, lulled into thinking their site had been saved that night. As it was, we would now be over our target before first light, find the flares, drop our bombs, and get out before the sun rose.

We were in a formation of six. Ahead of us were three more planes, the finders, and behind us was the main body of the squadron, over a hundred heavy bombers from squadrons across England. I found myself humming "Silent Night," but this was not going to be a holy night or a calm night. On the other hand, we were going to drop enough incendiaries to make it bright.

"Are the bombs fused and selected?" Jed asked.

"Fused and selected, ready for drop," Drew replied. "Our very own Christmas presents for the Krauts."

There was chuckling over the intercom from different people in different parts of the plane. I pictured the bombs.

The ground crew had "decorated" them, painting on bows and inscriptions like *Do not open until Christmas* and pretend name tags that read *For Hans.*

"Waiting for your mark to—"

"I'm getting echoes on the fishpond!" Jacko screamed out. "Coming hard and fast, coming from the ground … north by northeast … fifteen degrees."

"How many?" Jed demanded. "How many do you read?"

"Nine … no, ten … no, twelve."

"Can you determine their course? Are they on intercept?"

"I can't tell … maybe … I don't know … Wait, they're breaking off into two groups … no, three."

I knew that could mean they were heading in different directions for different targets, or it could also mean they were going to come at us from three directions.

"This is flight leader to formation," Jed said over the radio. "We're going to take some evasive action. Follow my course and altitude change. Davie, give us the course change *now*."

I read out the course change, and could already feel us gaining height. As I was giving the last coordinate, the plane started to bank sharply.

"What is their distance?" Jed asked. His voice was—as always—calm.

"Less than a mile and closing," Jacko reported. "They're

breaking off into pairs, but at least a few pairs are on an intercept course. They're coming after us."

"This is flight leader to squadron. All eyes open, prepare for contact."

There was nothing I could do as a navigator except add an extra set of eyes. I stood up, pushed aside the curtain, and stepped into the cockpit. I suddenly felt much more exposed. I *was* more exposed. All above me was the glass of the canopy. Anxiously I looked around, but I could see nothing but the black night sky, some thin clouds above, and more open sky with twinkling stars. I couldn't see anything that mattered.

"Closing from the back," Jacko screamed loudly.

"Tail end Charlie, be aware," Jed said over the radio. "Expect—"

"We have contact!" screamed a voice over the radio.

I looked back in time to see an enemy fighter plane zip past the last plane in our formation, bullets streaming out of it. More bullets were making their way toward it as our gunners returned fire! Then a second fighter appeared, and a third and a fourth! All four ducked and dodged between the Lancs before disappearing into the darkness.

"Anybody hit? Any damage?" Jed asked.

"Affirmative. This is CF8 and we've taken fire!" a voice

called out. "Some damage to my elevator, I think. The controls are floppy."

"Can you maintain—"

Tracers streamed by our starboard wing. A fighter came up from below and streaked by us, and our guns started firing, the pounding sound of shells, and I saw bullets chasing after it and—

"I got him!" Glen screamed, and at the same instant black smoke erupted from the engine of the fighter.

There were flames coming from the plane, allowing me to follow him as he slipped to the side … He slowed down … He was stalling. Jed banked sharply to port and the enemy vanished from my view, but he was going down, the pilot maybe already dead. That plane wasn't going to be worrying anybody anymore.

"Aircraft on the port quarter!" Glen yelled. "Coming fast and—"

"I see him!" Sandy screamed, and he began firing.

I saw tracer bullets flying through the air, and then saw and heard and felt as they tore into our port wing! The enemy plane disappeared, with bullets from Glen chasing after it.

"He missed the engine—I think," Jed yelled.

"More planes, more fighters, closing from behind and—"

There was an explosion and sparks flashed, and the whole plane staggered and shook. I had to grab on to the roof support to stop myself from tumbling over. There was a rush of air and the navigator's curtain blew in the breeze. Part of the canopy had been shot out! The plane started to dip violently and I was thrown forward into the back of Scottie's seat. He was covered with blood and the side of his head was gone.

Panicked, shocked, my stomach lurching into my throat, I tried to push myself away, but I couldn't. I was held in place by gravity as the plane continued to dive.

I yelled, "Jed, Jed, Scottie's been—"

But Jed was slumped forward over the yoke, a gash in the side of his head, blood seeping from a wound in his neck. We were going down!

23

My mind froze, as if I couldn't understand or believe what I was seeing, what was happening. Scottie and Jed were both dead or dying—at the very least unconscious—and the plane was going down. I had to do something, grab my parachute or—

Drew had been at his position in the nose cone, but now his head appeared beneath Scottie's inert body, and he started to push past him to get up and into the cockpit. There was a look of complete shock on his face and he was covered with blood as well! He was struggling, trying to climb up as the plane continued to scream down—we were gaining speed as we dove. If we didn't get out of it soon, we were all going to die! We had to level out if we were going to have even a chance of getting to the escape hatches. That was our only hope, and every second counted.

"Help me!" I screamed. "Help me!"

I grabbed Jed from behind and he yelled out in pain. He was alive! For a split second I stopped—I didn't want to hurt him—but then I began again. I had to pull him off the yoke or we were all dead.

Jed was big, and both his weight and the momentum of the plane made it almost impossible to dislodge him. Drew, who was still trying to climb up from below, wedged himself against Jed and started pushing him. As we hauled him back, I reached over and grabbed the yoke, yanking it as hard as I could with all my might, trying to pull us out of the dive.

There was so much force, so much momentum, that I couldn't pull it back. I strained with every inch of my being, every ounce of my strength, and slowly the plane started to react. The dive lessened just a bit, and then more and more. It was working. I kept pulling back until we were in a controlled descent, and then finally we flattened out.

"What's happening? What's happening!" Sandy yelled over the intercom from the tail of the plane.

"We've been hit! We've been hit!" Drew screamed. "Jed, Scottie—they're hurt!"

"Should we bail?" Jacko hollered.

"Affirmative!" Drew yelled. "Affirmative, get ready to—"

"No!" I screamed. "Do not bail!"

Drew glanced over at me. He looked crazed, panicked.

"Not yet! Help me get Jed out of the seat!" I yelled.

He didn't react, although I knew he must have heard me.

"Now, Drew! I need your help *now!*"

He started to pull Jed over and the whole plane began to bank to the port side.

"No, no, from the back!"

I kept one hand on the yoke and with the other fumbled around with Jed's safety harness until I undid the clasp. At the same time Drew unlatched the back of the pilot's seat, which folded down. He wrapped his arms around Jed's waist and pulled him. Jed was screaming in pain. At least we knew he was still alive, but for how long? There was so much blood.

As soon as Jed was clear, I dropped down into the seat, slammed the back up, and settled my feet onto the pedals. We were out of the dive and flying flat and level. The plane was now under my control. Out of habit I pushed the stick forward and the plane dipped slightly. I pulled back and levelled us off.

"This is Davie!" I called out over the intercom. "I'm at the controls!"

"Are we bailing? Are we bailing?" Jacko asked.

"No, not yet." I tried to make myself sound calm. I *needed* to be calm. "Jacko, are there any more fighters on the radar?"

"What?"

"Are there more fighters? Are we still in contact?"

"No, nothing, nothing ... they've left us for dead! We need to bail out!"

"I need you to stay calm," I said. "I need everybody to stay calm. Glen and Sandy, stay active. Keep your eyes open in case somebody is coming looking for us. Jacko, I need you in the cockpit, please."

I looked over my shoulder at Drew. He was hunched over Jed, whom he'd spread out along the floor.

"Drew, how is he? ... Is he ...?"

"It's his arm. A major artery was cut, but I've applied a tourniquet. The bleeding has almost stopped."

"And you—where were you hit?"

"I wasn't."

"But the blood—you're covered with blood."

"It's not mine."

Scottie ... I looked over. I saw again the gaping wound on the side of his head. Blood was splattered all over the canopy. His uniform was stained and soaked.

"Oh, my Lord," Jacko said as he appeared over my shoulder.

"I need you in the flight engineer's place," I said.

He hesitated for a split second and then responded. He undid Scottie's harness and eased him out of the seat. I tried not to look as his body flopped to the side, brushing against my leg. I held firm so as not to put pressure on the right pedal. Jacko slipped into his seat.

"I need to know our altitude, heading, and approximate position."

"We're at almost two thousand feet. We have enough height to bail out!"

"We've got time and altitude. What is our position?"

"What does it matter? We're somewhere over occupied France, so what does it matter?"

"It *does* matter. I can get us closer to home before we bail."

"Are you sure?"

"The controls are good and—" Just at that instant my eye was caught by flames on the port side!

"Fire in one of the port engines!" Glen screamed from the top turret.

I looked over. The inside port engine was on fire. I had to put out the fire!

"Jacko, do you see the four lights on the far right of the console?"

"Yes. Yes. One of them is red."

"That's the engine temp for the inside port engine."

Instinctively I reached over to the side. I pulled back

the throttle controlling the disabled engine—there was no point in feeding it fuel—while at the same time I pushed forward the throttle on the remaining port engine to compensate for the loss of power on that side.

"Right below it is a switch. There's a safety cover to protect it. I need you to flip it up and then push the button. It's the fire extinguisher for that engine. Do you understand?"

"Yes ... yes, I understand."

My eyes shot from the engine to him, and then, as he hit the switch, back to the engine as a stream of foam shot out. The flames died, as did the engine. We were now flying on three engines.

"I still need that heading."

"What?" Jacko questioned.

"The heading, give me our heading! What direction are we going?" I realized I wasn't sounding calm anymore.

"Oh, sorry. North by northeast."

"Okay, I'm going to have to bring us about. Everybody hold tight."

I executed a smooth, long bank, making sure not to stall or slow down or lose any altitude. We didn't have enough height to play with.

"Watch the compass. Let me know when we're on a

heading of exactly three thirty degrees south by southwest, okay?"

Jacko didn't say anything.

"Do you understand?" I screamed.

"Understood, yes ... We're coming around ... almost due north ... now northwest ... Okay, still coming, coming—"

"Just tell me when we're on the right heading," I said, cutting him off. "Drew, how is Jed doing?"

"The bleeding has stopped, but he's lost a lot of blood. He's barely conscious. I'm going to give him some morphine. He's in a lot of pain."

"Is there any chance he'll be able to jump?"

Drew didn't answer—which was an answer. Of course he couldn't jump, and even if he did and somehow survived the landing, there'd be no way he'd get the medical help he needed to live.

"Glen and Sandy, keep your eyes wide open. We have no radar and no wireless right now to warn us. If they're coming, they're going to be coming from above, so keep your eyes high."

"Okay, coming up to the mark," Jacko said.

I started to pull us out of the bank.

"And now!"

I levelled the plane out. "Okay, we're about two hours,

maybe a bit longer, from the coast. I'm going to hold us steady until then. Jacko, I need you to go back on the wireless, try to find a navigation beacon, get some air support, and let them know what's happening."

"Sure, mate." He got up from the seat.

"Drew, have you given Jed the morphine?"

"Just finished."

"Good. I need you to go below. We have to lighten the load."

"You want me to release the bombs?"

"Yes, it'll let us gain speed. The faster we get home, the faster we can get Jed help."

"Home?" he said incredulously. "What are you talking about? We have to bail out. We're down to three engines, and the captain is gone!"

"He's not *gone*. He's here and alive and I can't just leave him. He has only one chance, and that chance is me being able to land this plane!"

24

"What's our altitude?" I asked Drew.

"Forty-nine hundred. Still directly on course."

"Good, thanks."

We were flying just above an extensive bank of clouds that extended below us for hundreds of miles. I wanted to be in clear skies but have a place to hide if we were attacked. The plane was crippled and there was no way I had the skills to pilot any meaningful evasive action. We were nothing more than a limping, injured duck, easy pickings for any enemy fighter that happened upon us.

"How are you doing?" Drew asked.

"I'm fine, but my arms are tired. *All* of me is tired." I paused. "The controls are slow and floppy."

"What do you think is wrong?"

"We might have taken some damage to the tail ... maybe the rudders, maybe the elevators. Once it's light we can do a visual inspection."

"That won't be too long. And if we do have to bail, it's better in the light."

"Better, but still … How's Jed?"

"I'll check."

He got out of his seat and I felt even more alone and scared.

"His breathing is shallow, but his pulse is strong," he said when he came back. "He's unconscious, but that might have more to do with the morphine than anything else. I think he's comfortable."

I was so grateful he was still alive, but I knew that left me with no choice. I hated to admit it—even quietly to myself in my mind—but if Jed had died, I could have abandoned the plane. I didn't want to hit the silk, but really, could I land a Lancaster? Wasn't I just going to kill him and me both when we hit the deck? Did I really think I could—

My attention was caught by a line on the panel. One of the lights was red.

"Drew, the light on the console—is that an engine light?"

"It's engine four."

"Outside starboard. Can you tell what's wrong with it?"

"I'm not a flight engineer, but it looks like it's running too hot. The temperature gauge shows it's running much higher than the other two engines."

"Can you see any problem?" I asked as I peered out of the window at the engine.

"I can't see anything. It's not on fire, I don't see any—No, wait—there's some smoke coming out … not a lot, but some, definitely some. What does that mean? What do we do?"

"I don't know. Maybe we should … maybe we should … reduce the power to that engine, not run it as hard. Does that make sense?"

"I guess so. We can run on two engines if we need to … right?"

"Yes, we can fly with two engines. I read that in the manuals." I paused. "Have you ever seen a Lancaster flying with only two engines?"

"No, but if the manuals say we can, then we can."

"Okay, then let's throttle back a little on that engine and add some throttle to the inside starboard."

I put my hand on the throttles. With my fingers I pulled the throttle back on the one engine while simultaneously using my thumb to increase the throttle on the other. I felt the plane's attitude change and I compensated with the yoke to level us out and—

"It's on fire! There are flames coming out of the outside engine!"

Without saying a word, I reached over and flipped up the cover and hit the fire extinguisher. I watched as the foam streamed out, smothering the flames. The plane suddenly slowed and slumped. I thrust forward the throttles on the two remaining engines, pushing them past the gate until they were almost all the way to the wall.

"We're still flying," Drew said.

"You sound surprised."

"Aren't you?"

"A little."

"Jacko, can you update us on position?" Drew asked.

"I can give you a rough plotting. I wish we had a navigator to do it right."

"So do I," I agreed.

"I think we'd better keep him up front," Drew said. "If you want to take the flight engineer's spot, I'll try to plot a course."

"Let's just keep a few of us in spots where we know what we're doing," Jacko replied. "I have a pretty good reckoning at just over one hundred and thirty miles from the coast."

"At our present airspeed we'll make the Channel in about twenty ... no, twenty-five minutes," I said.

We were almost home. A short skip across the Channel and then we'd be over England. When the crew bailed, they'd be in friendly hands—they'd be safe. Then it would just be Jed and me in the plane when I tried to bring it down.

"We have company!" Jacko yelled out. "Echoes on the fishpond!"

I started us down toward the clouds. We couldn't outrun anything, but I had to hope that we could dive into the clouds and play possum and—

"It's Spitfires!" Jacko yelled. "It's Spits! It's our guys! I've got them on the radio—patching you through, Skip!"

I felt such a rush of relief that tears came to my eyes. I tried to snuffle them back. I pulled back on the yoke to keep us above the clouds. I was happier to be able to see where we were flying.

"This is Spitfire leader to Lancaster pilot." It was a distinctly English accent.

"This is the Lancaster pilot. You won't believe how happy we are to hear your voice."

"We're rather pleased to speak to you as well. We'll make sure you're safe and secure all the way home."

I wished he could take me all the way to my real home— in Canada.

"Does anybody see them?" I asked over the intercom.

"Nothing," Glen said from the top turret. "Still too dark."

"I'm starting to see the sun coming up behind us," Sandy added. "It'll soon catch us, especially at this speed."

"That's the only thing I'm happy to be caught by," I said.

It was almost light and we were under the protection of our fighters. The coast was almost in sight and we'd soon be over the English countryside and safe ... Well, at least some of us would be safe.

The light from the rising sun started to stream in through the top of the canopy. I could see now that there were multiple holes in the canopy, one smaller panel of glass was shattered, and blood was splattered all along the starboard-side window. Drew had done his best with material and adhesive tape from the first aid kit to cover up as many of the holes as possible. His repairs had blocked off some of the air entering the cockpit but didn't completely stop the flow of bitter, freezing wind. My whole body was cold and numb. I flexed my fingers repeatedly, trying to keep them supple and able to work the controls.

In the growing light I could now see members of our escort. There were two Spitfires off our port side, just ahead and above, and another pair high and off to the starboard. We were now safe from enemy attack.

"Glennie, Sandy, you can stand down."

"Thanks, Skipper."

Skipper—that was so familiar and so strange at the same time, because they were talking to *me*.

The sunlight had completely caught up to us. Daylight had arrived. I hoped that the rays would start to warm the cockpit a bit. I could also get some warmth by dropping down to a lower elevation, but I needed to do one thing before that.

"Spitfire leader, this is Lancaster pilot requesting a visual inspection."

"Affirmative on that request," he replied.

The lead Spit dropped back and dipped until he was sitting no more than fifteen yards off my port wing.

"I would imagine you're aware that you're only running on two engines," he said.

"We did notice that," I replied.

"Just thought I should mention it. There are also numerous bullet holes in your wing and some other marks visible on the main fuselage."

He reduced his airspeed and dropped back again until he was sitting right off our tail.

"Do you have full rudder and elevator?" he asked.

"It's a bit sluggish."

"I would imagine that would be the case since your right rudder is full of holes and it appears that part of your elevator is no longer attached to your aircraft."

I didn't know what to say.

"You've done remarkably well, chaps, to get this bird home. Ten more minutes and you'll reach the coast, and then another fifteen and you're over friendly territory. I want you to fall in behind me and we'll lead you home."

"Appreciated."

The Spitfire came back alongside and the pilot waved. I waved back. It did feel reassuring to have somebody else not only by our side but plotting the course, and now leading the way.

"Lancaster leader, are you planning on attempting a landing or looking for a place to bail?"

"Both," I said.

"Both? I don't understand."

"We're going to have crew members hit the silk before I attempt to land."

"Not quite the vote of confidence I'd want from my crew if I was the pilot," he answered.

"That's the problem. I'm not the pilot. I'm the navigator."

There was a pause at the other end. "Please, say again that message."

"I'm the navigator."

Again there was no instant response. "Have you ever landed a plane?" he asked.

"Negative."

"Lancaster, um, pilot, would you consider having all crew members including yourself bail out and abandoning the craft?"

"Negative. We have an injured crew member who is not capable of abandoning the plane. I have to attempt a landing."

"Understood ... and respected. Please stay on my tail and I'll get you home."

I was glad he understood and glad he respected the decision, but really, what choice did I have?

25

I made a big circle of the field. I could see the runways, the buildings, the trees alongside, and in the distance the village and the Anglican church, its spire rising high into the sky. It was all so familiar, all so good to see. I thought of all the times I'd flown back in after a mission—twenty-three times before—and how welcome a sight it always was. This was what I had been silently praying for the whole return trip, all I'd wanted, just to get back here. But now that I was here, I knew I was much more than simply at the end of my journey. I was possibly, simply, at the end.

"This is control tower. Preparations on the ground are complete."

I knew all about the preparations. On our last pass I'd seen the heat and meat trucks—the fire trucks along with six waiting ambulances. One was for Jed. The other five were for the rest of the crew.

"You are clear to have crew begin evacuation. Commence on your next pass."

"Affirmative."

I turned to Drew, still sitting in the flight engineer's seat. "Altitude?" I asked.

"Fifteen hundred feet."

Right behind me, Jacko, Glen, and Sandy were all standing, chutes attached to their harnesses, ready to jump. Drew had his chute beside him on the floor, ready to hook onto his harness.

At their feet was Jed. He was quiet and comfortable, the morphine dulling the pain, his vital signs strong, the bleeding stopped. Jacko, who had received first aid training, thought he was stable and was going to make it—assuming I could get him down to the ground. Scottie's body had been moved to the back and covered—wrapped in his parachute, out of respect.

"Okay, I'm going to bring us around again, right over the field," I said. "Get ready to jump."

Jacko put a hand on my shoulder. "Skip, thanks for what you did ... You got us back home."

"Yeah, without you we would have gone down over France, one way or another," Glen agreed.

"I was just doing what had to be done," I said.

"Maybe we should all stay with the plane," Sandy added.

"No, you shouldn't!" I exclaimed. "I need you all to leave. All of you, now … please."

"I think he's just afraid to join the Caterpillar Club," Jacko said. "Come on, mate, I'll promise to hold your hand all the way down."

"We're coming around in less than thirty seconds. You all have to get to the door."

There were three slaps on the back and then Drew got up from the flight engineer's seat. "Your wheels are down and locked."

"Thanks. Thanks for being there beside me," I said.

"Thank *you*. I'm alive because of what you did."

"I just want you to *stay* alive. Go now, please."

He reached over and offered me his hand. I took one hand off the yoke and we shook.

"I'll see you on the ground," I said.

"I'm counting on it."

"Okay, *go*."

He clipped on his chute and rushed toward the hatch.

I levelled out of the bank and brought us in flat and slow. I kept it straight the whole length of the field. When I'd cleared the field, I banked to avoid the church steeple at the end of the runway. And as I made the bank, I caught sight of a chute! And then a second and a third and … where was the fourth? I banked harder to keep the chutes in sight. There were still only three. Had the fourth chute malfunctioned? Had somebody plummeted to the ground?

"Hey, Skip." It was Drew!

"What are you doing here?" I exclaimed.

"I decided to stay with the ship." He sat down in the flight engineer's seat. "I thought you might have a better shot at landing this crate with the help of a flight engineer."

"But you're not a flight engineer."

"Yeah, and you're not really a pilot, but I won't mention that again if you don't mention that 'not a flight engineer' stuff again."

"Drew, you have to jump."

"I'm not going anywhere, mate, and I don't think you can make me, unless you're planning on leaving the yoke and trying to toss me out."

"Look, I appreciate what you're doing, but—"

"This is the control tower," came a voice over the radio. "We have three on the ground, all good. Wasn't there going to be a fourth?"

"Negative, control tower," Drew said before I could answer. "This is the acting flight engineer. We felt it was better if we had both a pilot and a flight engineer."

"Affirmative on that. Winds are coming from due north

at eleven miles per hour, with gusts to fifteen. Be aware of crosswinds and you are cleared for landing."

"Roger that," Drew replied. He turned to me. "So, let's go down and say hello to the guys."

I needed to bring us around in a big, big circle, lose about a thousand feet, and head straight into the runway from the east. I pushed down hard on the yoke. The controls had become increasingly sluggish, but the plane still responded and we started to descend. Up ahead I could clearly see the lane formed by the green path-indicator lights. I put us right in the middle.

"Eight hundred ... seven hundred and fifty ... seven ... You have to get down lower or we'll have to make another pass."

I pressed down even harder and we dropped faster.

"Good, there's the steeple, straight ahead."

The runway lined up perfectly with the steeple. It was an obstacle when we were taking off in that direction and a marker coming in this way.

"Five hundred ... four-seventy ..."

"What's my airspeed?"

"One-eighty ... Do you want me to throttle back?"

"No, no, I don't want to stall it out, better to come in fast."

I suddenly realized that I was drifting off line for the runway. I turned the wheel and worked the rudder and we adjusted, but too fast and too far! My heart rushed up into my throat and I pressed back the other way to self-correct until my nose was right in line with the centre of the runway.

"You never landed a plane before, right?" Drew asked.

"Well ... sort of ... once."

"Sort of?"

"It was a Link Trainer."

"At least that's something."

"Not really. I crashed it."

He laughed. "Is it too late for me to jump?"

"What's our height?" I asked.

"One hundred and ninety ... A little late, but don't worry, I know you can do it."

"Yeah, right, thanks for at least pretending."

"No pretending—I'm betting my life on it. Ninety feet ... eighty feet ... sixty ... Pull up your nose and get the rear wheel to hit first."

I adjusted the elevators and the altitude changed. I reached over and pulled the throttles back, reducing the fuel, reducing the speed, and the sound of the engine diminished.

"Come on, Davie, nice and easy, just clear the fence, you can do it."

We cruised in, barely above the fence, and then the

runway was underneath us, and we hit against the deck hard and I bounced out of my seat. I pushed the yoke forward and the plane jerked and tipped up, the tires screeching against the pavement before it righted itself!

"Throttle down, throttle down!" I screamed.

Drew grabbed the throttles and pulled them back, and I squeezed the brakes and the plane started veering off to the side of the tarmac. I squeezed harder on the other side to bring it back in line, but it wasn't working! We rumbled off the pavement and onto the grass, and the whole plane started bouncing and pitching so much that I thought it was going to get airborne again. I squeezed the brakes so hard I thought they were going to break off, but it was slowing down at last, more and more. Finally, the Lancaster came to a stop. There was complete silence.

I looked over at Drew.

"I've seen better landings," he said.

"What?" I asked in disbelief.

"You're supposed to try to keep the plane *on* the pavement. I'll forgive you this once, but I expect better things of you the next time."

He started laughing and I joined in. It was either that or start crying.

26

"He's expecting you," the clerk said as I walked into the office.

"Thanks."

"Just go right in," he said. "By the way, that really was some fine flying."

"Thanks." I'd been hearing that a lot, but to me it still seemed like simple dumb luck that I'd been able to land that plane.

"You should be very proud of what you did, regardless," he went on.

What exactly did *that* mean?

I stopped in front of the CO's door. Even though I'd been told to go right in, I knocked and waited for a response.

"Come!"

I opened the door, walked in, and closed it behind me. "Reporting as requested, sir," I said and saluted.

He waved back a reluctant return salute. "Sit. Did you manage to get any sleep?" Group Captain Matthews asked.

"A little, sir," I replied as I sat down. "I kept getting interrupted, men coming around to congratulate me."

"Well-deserved congratulations. That plane was so beaten up that it was a miracle you were able to get her back to base to begin with. I have no idea how you managed to fly it with almost all of your elevator missing."

"I knew it was missing a piece in flight, but I would imagine that most of it fell off when I hit the deck. It was a pretty hard landing. It wasn't exactly textbook, sir."

"Any landing that you can walk away from is a good one."

"Speaking of walking away, sir, can you update me on Jed—I mean, Flight Lieutenant Blackburn?"

"As you know, after he was stabilized, he was transferred to the hospital at district headquarters for surgery."

"And is there word on him yet, sir?"

"There is." He smiled and I felt my heart melt. "He's going to pull through."

I suddenly burst into tears. "Sorry, sir, I'm just so ... I shouldn't be ..."

"It's all right, son. Tears of joy and tears of relief and maybe even some tears of gratitude."

He got up, circled the desk, pulled out a handkerchief, and handed it to me.

"He's alive because of you, son."

"I had help, sir, lots of help."

"You were the one behind the yoke. It seems you got your wish to be a pilot sooner than you thought you might."

"Yes, sir."

"I guess you're used to doing things a little earlier than you should, aren't you?" he asked.

"Umm ... maybe sometimes, sir."

"Definitely sometimes. I was hoping you could help me with a little problem, a little confusion I'm experiencing."

"If I can, sir." I wasn't sure what he could possibly mean by that.

He picked up a piece of paper from his desk. "Late yesterday I received a cable from the Royal Canadian Mounted Police. It concerns a missing boy."

"A missing boy?" I repeated, my voice cracking over the last word.

"It says the *boy*—and he is a *boy*, because he's not yet eighteen—was discovered missing by his mother. Apparently she went to visit him at his boarding school—she'd heard he was sick. But he wasn't there."

All of the blood drained from my face, and I felt a rush of fear that was worse than anything I'd experienced in the plane.

"And by the strangest coincidence, this boy has the *same* last name as you. And even stranger, he has the same mother and father as you. Wouldn't you say that was an incredible coincidence ... Robert?"

I was caught. There was no way out. "I'm so sorry, sir. It all just ... just happened."

He shook his head. "I don't know whether I should preside over a court martial and throw you in the stockade because you're a fraud, or decorate you because you're a hero. The problem with the latter is that I'm really not sure what name to put on the medal." He paused. "It *is* Robert, isn't it?"

"Yes, sir. David is my—"

I was interrupted by loud noises, yelling coming from the outer office, and suddenly the door burst open and in walked Drew, Jacko, Glen, and Sandy.

"Sorry to disturb you, sir!" Jacko yelled out. "But we need to talk to you."

"All four of you get out immediately!" he ordered. "This is not the time or place."

"Afraid it is both the time *and* the place," Jacko replied. "We came here to tell you that Davie here is a hero— that none of us would be standing here if it hadn't been for him!"

"I believe I'm fully aware of what he did, but there are things that—"

"No disrespect, sir, but we want you to know that we are all equally responsible for the trouble Davie is in," Drew said.

"How do you know that McWilliams is in trouble?" Group Captain Matthews asked.

"There aren't many secrets on this base, sir. We heard that Davie was in trouble, sir," Drew replied.

"And we're all responsible," Jacko added.

"Do you even know what he's in trouble for?" the commander asked. He turned to me, holding out a finger. "And not a word from you!"

"Well, sir, there's just so much, I don't know where to begin," Jacko said. "But what we do know is that he's a genuine hero and he needs to be given a medal!"

"Robert, would you like to explain it to them?"

They all looked at each other.

"Robert? Who's Robert?" Glen asked.

I raised my hand. "I'm Robert."

"And you should know that Robert is not only not who he claimed to be, he is not the age he claimed to be. He is just seventeen years old."

All four men looked shocked.

"He enlisted under a false name while underage. Do you know what that means?" the commander asked.

"That the air force needs more seventeen-year-old pilots?" Jacko guessed.

For a split second the commander looked as though he was at a loss for words.

Jacko pushed on. "Sir, I appreciate—I think we all appreciate—that regardless of the circumstances that brought Davie—I mean Robert—here, what he did makes him a hero."

"Yeah, you can't throw him in the stockade!" Drew said.

"I wasn't planning on throwing him in the stockade."

"That's more like it!" Jacko exclaimed.

"But I'm about *this* close to tossing *you* in detention," he said, holding his finger and thumb just a fraction apart.

Jacko shut his mouth and looked down at his feet.

"Robert is not going to be jailed," the CO said.

I felt a rush of relief.

"But he's also not going back into a plane," he continued. "Instead, he will be going back to Canada, to Toronto, to complete his school year. And when he turns eighteen years of age in July, he *will* re-enlist and be sent to flight school, where he will be trained to become a pilot."

"I'm going to be a pilot!" I exclaimed.

"Not just a pilot, son, but a *Lancaster* pilot. At the time of your qualification as a pilot, you will be reassigned to this squadron, where you will be expected to complete the remaining six missions of your tour."

"That's ... that's incredible, sir!"

"There is no need to call me sir anymore. You are no longer a member of this squadron, or, for that matter, a member of the Royal Canadian Air Force. You and your medal are going home."

"Thank you! Thank you so much!"

"I don't know if you should be thanking me. You may have faced enemy fighters and flak over here, but you're about to go home to face the music ... and your mother."

"Do you think you could just throw me in the stockade instead?" I asked, and everybody broke into laughter.

"Now, I want all five of you to get out of my office before I throw *somebody* in the stockade."

Everybody scrambled for the door.

"Wait!" he called out, and we all froze. "Robert will be flying home tomorrow evening. Until then, you four are responsible for him."

"Of course, no problem, we'll take great care of him!" Jacko answered. The grin on his face was a mile wide, and the CO must have noticed.

"Yes, you'll take wonderful care of this seventeen-year-old *boy*—a boy who is too young to drink—and you'll return him to this office by fifteen hundred hours tomorrow afternoon. Understood?"

"Understood, sir," Drew said.

I went to leave and then stopped. There was one more thing I wanted to do before I was kicked out of the air force. I turned to Captain Matthews.

"It's been an honour to serve under you, sir," I said, and saluted.

He stood and returned my salute. "And it's been an *honour* to have you as a member of my squadron, McWilliams. You are dismissed ... And don't let me catch you here again until you're actually, truthfully, and genuinely eighteen years old!"

A message for my readers
from Eric Walters

I *love* writing. While I'm glad when teachers and other adults like my books, I'm even happier when children and young adults like them. Those are the people I write for. When I was a teacher I read each of my books to my students while I was writing them to find out what they liked, what they didn't like, what confused them, and to help me become a better writer. Now, writing full-time and out of the classroom, there's a danger of a gap growing between me and my readers. I want to close the gap. I really want to know what *you* think of this book.

What did you like, what didn't you like, what would have made the book better, and what do you think I should write about next? Email me at ericwalters@uniserve.com and let me know.

I promise that I will read your email and use that information to help me become better at writing books that you want to read. Your opinion doesn't just matter to me—it matters a lot.

Eric

ONE TEEN. ONE DESERT.
ONE EPIC JOURNEY.

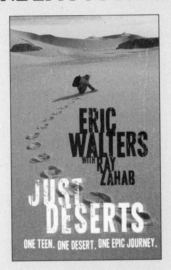

"Dear Ethan:
I know you must be terribly confused, a little bit scared and thinking,
hoping, praying, that the plane will return. It will not."

Ethan can barely believe it. Until now, his biggest problems have
been trying to stay in one school without getting expelled. But now
his father has stepped in with a shockingly drastic measure and
Ethan finds himself sprawled in the sand.
In the Sahara Desert. Alone.

penguin.ca

How many
ERIC WALTERS
books have you read?